THE
NAKED DEMON

Published by True Will Publishing

ISBN 978-1-84396-703-3

Also available as a Kindle ebook
ISBN 978-1-84396-704-0

A catalogue record for this book is available
from the British Library and American Library of Congress

Cover design by Adrian Dobbie.

Also by Trevor Gray

A WHISPER IN THE SILENCE
An inspiring naturist love story

A private desert island in the middle of the Pacific Ocean. A deep-thinking multi-millionaire seeking solitude, silence and a naturist lifestyle.

The unexpected arrival of a beautiful young glamour model in need of Prosecco and noisy parties.

Mismatch, humour, spiritual wisdom, near tragedy and all-conquering love. One unforgettable heart-warming tale.

★★★★★ Lovely Read

What a lovely romantic novel. Equally great for relaxing on the beach or cosying in on the couch on a blustery autumn day. Myth busting, positive portrayal of naturism and absolutely bursting with quotes and interesting information. Well written and very enjoyable. Loved it!

★★★★★ Enriching love story with an overall sense of good feeling

I was fortunate enough to come across a copy of Trevor Gray's first book 'From Manhood To Godhood' so was surprised to see another book available so quickly.

This is quite different from the first, but it is a beautiful story told with insight and humour and filled with spirituality and 'feelgood' factor. I cannot recommend this book enough for anyone who wishes to explore a new author, a great story and themselves. I would urge everyone to read it.'

★★★★★ **Silence IS Golden**

Love, laughter, deep meditation, much about truth, little about consequences, intuition runs rampant as the reader is pulled in a fantastic naturist tale of wonderment.

TRUE WILL PUBLISHING

This book is dedicated to
to Rosie, my wife and soulmate, and to my
brother Brian and sister Veronica.

With special thanks to Adrian for
his cover design, to John for his typesetting
and pre-press production, and to
Rosie, Lynda and Grant for their proofreading.

THE
NAKED DEMON

Trevor Gray

TRUE WILL PUBLISHING

1

'It's Jason,' the voice on the phone said. 'I know it's the middle of the night, but this is urgent. You're under attack!'

Liam was shocked and for a moment speechless. He knew his best friend would not have disturbed their sleep unless he was serious. Jason was an astute and enlightened individual, a senior member of a respected magical fraternity.

'What on earth makes you say that?' he asked, mystified.

'Call it the gift of knowing, but I'm absolutely certain,' came the immutable reply. 'Someone has it in for you and Faye. They won't stop until they've succeeded.'

Hearing this made Liam even more anxious. 'But who would want to harm either of us, especially my girlfriend?' She was his prime concern.

'I've no idea at the moment,' Jason admitted. 'There's the possibility Faye could be their main target. The assaults could be physical, psychological, or maybe psychic attacks. They might even be a hate crime. I'll use all my expertise to try and find out. In the meantime, what are you intending to do today?'

'We were thinking of going to the naturist beach.' Even as he said it, he was wondering if it was such a good idea.

'Would it be alright, taking into account what you've just told me?'

There was a slight pause at the other end, but not out of surprise, as Jason and Scarlet, his own girlfriend, were nudists too.

He was obviously weighing up the situation. 'I guess it'll be as safe or risky as anywhere else. Staying in your flat could be even worse. Sorry I can't be more specific, but we'll speak again later. Just make sure you're extremely careful.'

It was no wonder neither Liam nor Faye could get back to sleep.

He had considered keeping quiet about Jason's premonition, but decided it was only fair to tell her. Not wanting to unnecessarily cause her stress however, he omitted the possibility of her being the main victim.

The awful thing was knowing they could be in danger but not being able to identify or confront it. In trying to make sense of the situation, their minds kept leaping to worse case scenarios. They imagined all sorts of possible threats, some of them ridiculous. One moment they concluded they were overacting; the next, even more gruesome thoughts would surface.

By the morning they were feeling just as helpless, but none the wiser.

The only distinct change was in the weather. The sound of thunder rumbled in the distance and a howling wind battered the bedroom window. They had heard the deteriorating conditions of course but had been too busy thinking about Jason's warning.

The weather forecast had been completely wrong. It had promised unbroken sunshine, not just for the city of Brighton, but for the whole South Coast.

Liam's heart sank even further as he opened the curtains and peered outside. The sky was dark and angry, the rain incessant.

'It's pouring,' he moaned. 'Not beach weather at all.'

Faye joined him, immediately agreeing with his assessment. 'I see what you mean. It's more like mid-winter than June.'

He pulled her close, putting a protective arm around her shoulder. 'In other words, just a typical English summer's day.'

They made a good couple. He was slim and good looking, 28 years of age, medium height, with light brown hair. Always dressed casually, when wearing anything at all, he had been born along the coast in Littlehampton. As a committed naturist, Brighton's designated beach had been one of the deciding factors, when he moved to the city a few years before.

She was slightly shorter than him and a couple of years younger. A stunningly beautiful brunette, with a to-die-for figure, she hailed from London. She had moved south to live with him just months earlier.

Her alluring sexy looks were slightly deceptive. Hidden behind them was a very sensitive being who lacked self-esteem. Being so dependent on him, she relished the genuine love and care he bestowed upon her.

Consistently the optimist, Liam as always decided to remain positive. One thing the weather could not do was to dampen his spirits. Come rain or shine and despite Jason's distressing phone call, he was determined their day would not be wasted. 'Perhaps we were not meant to go to the beach today.' He had already come up with an alternative. 'We can go to the naturist health spa instead. It's been a while since we were last there.'

Faye was not against going, but crowded saunas made her self-conscious. This was especially so when they were mainly full of men. 'Let's make it nice and early. Hopefully, we'll have the place to ourselves.'

As far as Liam was concerned, the sooner the better. 'It opens at noon, so we'll have some breakfast and then get a cab.'

Their minds were made up. An enjoyable day was back on the cards, or so they thought. Little did they know that it was impossible for them to escape the onset of evil which Jason had predicted.

Their lives were about to change forever. Nothing would ever be the same again.

As they settled the fare and climbed out of the taxi, a female member of staff was unlocking the front door to reception.

They were greeted warmly, as they always had been in the past.

Paying the entrance fee and being given a locker key and fluffy towels, they made their way through to the changing room. There they undressed.

Liam, always keen to strip off his clothes, loved this naturist health spa, where no silly swimming costumes were allowed. Faye was equally delighted, her reason being that they were the only customers so far.

As they descended the stairs, the immediate increase in temperature banished all thoughts of the inclement weather outside. It reminded them instead of the sensation you get when stepping off a plane in the Canary Islands or some other hot destination.

All they had to do now was choose from all the wonderful facilities on offer. There were saunas, steam rooms, a jacuzzi, a small swimming pool and several inviting hot tubs.

After taking a shower, they opted for the largest of the latter. Blue tiled walls enclosed the tub on three sides, the opening at the front having access steps.

Entering this inviting oasis, they lowered themselves onto the built-in seats, Faye to one side and Liam at the front. Sitting comfortably, their heads just above the buoyant, silky soft water, they took deep breaths, inhaling the calming, soothing scents. The aromatherapy oils masked any trace of spa sanitisers or water treatments. Their nostrils were instead delighted by the fragrance of opulent perfumes.

Through lack of sleep, low lighting and the peaceful ambiance of gentle instrumental music, they soon drifted into a pleasant, serene state of relaxed drowsiness.

Suddenly, Liam was aware of Faye's leg nudging him.

Stirring, he discovered a man sitting opposite her.

Liam, being right next to the entrance steps, could not understand how the newcomer had entered the hot hub unnoticed. Almost impossible, it made no sense.

The stranger's attire was even more extraordinary. Although partly submerged, he was fully clothed in a long-sleeved shirt, dark trousers and even a pair of shoes. To be dressed this way in water was ludicrous. It was also completely inappropriate for a naturist venue.

Of massive build, the giant of a being was bald headed, his skin pale and acned.

He sat motionless, his bulging eyes locked menacingly into Faye's. Had he been ogling her attractive naked body it would have been understandable, albeit disrespectful. Instead, it was only her eyes he seemed interested in.

Faye felt extremely uncomfortable about this unnerving intrusion. She hated being stared at. It really did her head in. So much so, that it had become a phobia.

She tried averting her own eyes, but they would not move.

Neither could she close them, to shut out his glare. They were locked in a wide-open position.

His gaze was cold and penetrating. It suggested questioning. His head being slightly tilted to one side, made his crazy eyes even more threatening.

Her anxiety increasing, she desperately tried to turn away.

She was paralysed. Her entire body was incapable of any movement.

The fiend's manic gaze intensified. It was ceaseless, predatory and deadly.

Petrified, shivers ran down her spine, defying the heat of the water.

Never once did the fiend blink. His eyelids were static, as he peered at her maliciously.

Dread-filled, with cheeks burning, tears streamed down Faye's face. Dry-mouthed, her stomach cramped with debilitating nausea.

Liam should have intervened sooner, but only then was he fully aware of what was happening. 'Stop looking at my girlfriend,' he demanded of the maniac.

It only intensified the hostile wide-eyed stare.

By now, Faye was trembling uncontrollably. Visibly quaking from head to toe, her heartbeat pounded dangerously.

Liam tried again. 'Stop staring at her now!' he yelled, 'Can't you see what it's doing to her?'

The piercing eyes never wavered. Defiantly, they bore even deeper into her soul.

In frenzied terror she tried to scream, but distress sealed her throat.

Outraged at the brute's cruelty Liam sprang to his feet.

With all his might, his hands scooped a massive wave of water, directly into the evil man's face. 'Do as I say! Stop staring at her, you bastard!'

The sadist arose slowly and menacingly to his feet.

His eyes moved from Faye to Liam. Aggressive and intimidating, his pose suggested fury.

Now it was Liam who felt threatened, but he was determined not to show it. Adrenaline flooded his bloodstream. It was fight or flight.

The latter option was discarded immediately, despite his hatred of violence.

His physical and emotional strength enhanced, he clenched his fists and took a deep breath.

Then it happened.

The ogre simply VANISHED! He disappeared. He was gone.

Liam could not believe his eyes, Frantically, he searched the water, where the man had been standing.

There was no trace of him.

'What the hell?' he tried to reason. 'No one can dematerialize like that. This is a hot tub, not some stage magician's illusion prop.'

Faye too had witnessed the sudden and impossible disappearance. Terrified that she was losing her sanity, she had reached breaking point.

As Liam continued his search, by now outside the hot tub, she crashed into a full-blown panic attack.

Pain crushed her chest. Like an icy hand it squeezed at her heart.

Choking, trauma gripped her throat, as her lungs spasmed.

Dread-filled, she gasped for air, unable to breathe.

Blood drained from her face. She felt she was dying.

Everything around began to spin, faster and faster and faster.

Dizziness plunged her into unconsciousness.

Slowly, her head sank beneath the surface of the water.

Faye was drowning!

2

'So, Ms King,' the psychiatrist began, turning his seat to face her full on, 'you've had another of your panic attacks.'

Faye felt herself blush. Suffering medical conditions such as this embarrassed her. 'I'm afraid so. Early yesterday afternoon. It wasn't my fault at all but caused by a disappearing man in a hot tub.'

Such a ridiculous statement did not surprise Dr Wright at all. He was well used to patients telling him the most ludicrous things. More time wasting. 'You'd better explain.'

She did her best to describe what had happened, how the man had appeared from nowhere, almost frightened her to death by staring into her eyes and then vanished into thin air.

The doctor glanced at his laptop screen. 'Your medical records suggest you most likely imagined everything. It was almost certainly a psychotic episode.'

Faye was quite offended by his immediate rejection and rebuttal of what she had told him. 'I was telling you the truth.' She had no idea anyway what *psychotic* meant.

He noted her bewildered look. 'A psychotic episode is when one perceives or interprets reality in a completely different way to others around them. Think of it as a hallucination or daydream. You were seeing something which was not actually there.'

Faye had been referred to Dr Wright several times since moving from London to Brighton. He was the resident psychiatrist at the local medical centre. One of the General Practitioners had first suggested she should see him.

In his late fifties, with greying hair, he was always dressed in the same old-fashioned looking suit. She had taken an instant dislike to his arrogant know-it-all manner. With a lack of empathy, he was cynical, humourless and tactless. It seemed as if he had no idea how to properly respond to referrals. To make matters worse, he always spoke extremely loudly. Their private and confidential conversations must have been overheard by the entire surgery.

A quick look around the room, which always smelt of perspiration, revealed it was the same as ever. Nothing had changed. There was no comfy couch, or even soft chairs for clients to relax on. Hard plastic ones were the only option. Two were brown, the other blue.

Most of the money, squeezed from tight Health Service budgets, had obviously been spent on Dr Wright's executive pedestal desk. Pushed up against the wall, she could count at least nine drawers, all with shiny brass handles. His black leather chair had swivel wheels, a reclining backrest and a retractable footrest. At least he was comfortable.

The only other furniture were three grey filing cabinets,

one of which had a printer on, a small wastebasket and a shelf lined with reference books.

'What I told you was true,' she tried to convince him. 'My boyfriend, Liam, was there. He witnessed everything, just as I've described. He also prevented me from drowning, lifting me from the water in seconds. The staff at the health spa were wonderful. They offered to call an ambulance, but it wasn't necessary.'

Having already made his assessment, the psychiatrist adjusted it slightly, adding information. 'Although it's rare, there is such a psychiatric phenomenon known as shared psychosis or shared delusional disorder. It's where two people experience the same delusional beliefs. Some refer to it as Folie à Deux, which is French for madness of two.'

Faye crossed her arms in a huff. Now he was suggesting that she and Liam were both mad.

She remembered something important. 'After I'd recovered, the staff at the health spa told us that we'd been the only customers there at the time.'

Hearing this, the look he gave her was contemptuous. 'Which proves my point completely. If there was no one else there, you must have imagined the whole thing.'

'No. Not at all,' she tried again, her face crumbling. 'You don't understand. You're missing the point.'

'I think not.' He had wasted enough time on her silly story. 'Listen carefully. You might learn something. Close relationships with strong emotional bonding can contribute to the possibility of shared psychosis. How long have you and your boyfriend been living together?'

He had asked her this before, at a previous consultation

but had obviously forgotten. 'It's about eight months now.'

'And how did you first meet?' He was probing.

She felt as if she was being interrogated but felt compelled to answer. 'I was with two of my friends. We had been for a drink at the West Quay pub in the Marina and decided to walk back along the seashore to Brighton Pier. Out of curiosity, we sat down on the naturist beach. We were clothed of course. That's when I first spotted Liam. He was extremely good-looking. I could hardly take my eyes off him. We started chatting and I found he was so easy to get on with. He had an awesome sense of humour and made me laugh. Although he was sitting there completely nude, he made it seem as if it was the most natural thing in the world. When my friends said they had to go, I decided to stay a while longer with him.'

Wright was typing notes on his laptop. 'Did you remove your own clothes?'

'Of course,' she affirmed with a nod. 'It seemed the right thing to do. With everyone else naked on the beach, I felt a bit awkward being the only one fully dressed.'

'But you must have felt embarrassed,' he supposed, 'showing Liam and everyone else your naked body, especially your private parts.'

Faye wondered why on earth he would think so. 'Not at all. As I explained the last time I saw you, I used to be a model. As it was mainly glamour photography, I was used to being nude. It was only when my problem started that I couldn't do the work anymore. I found I was suffering from—'

'Scopophobia,' he interrupted, 'the fear of being stared

at or watched. It was this which contributed to you first having panic attacks.'

'They came on unexpectedly,' she could remember clearly. 'I began to get upset about people looking at me and photographers snapping pictures. I realised it was only my looks they were interested in.'

'Has it never occurred to you, young lady, that being naked in public is the worst thing anyone can do?' He was so patronising. 'Of course it's going to make people stare at you. It's common sense.'

'No, it's not,' she countered, determined to put him right. 'People don't always stare. A few weeks ago, Liam took me away to a wonderful naturist resort in Gran Canaria. It was lovely and we had an amazing time. Although everyone was naked, they were all just happily relaxing by the pool in the sun. Everyone was nice and friendly, but no one stared at me at all. This is what you don't understand, genuine naturists don't gaze at each other, not even here in Brighton.'

'That's twaddle,' he maintained. 'I don't approve of public nudity, wherever it is. The council should do the right thing and close the naturist beach immediately.'

'It's been here for well over forty years,' she enlightened him. 'There was an article about it in the Evening Argus. Apparently, it's brought the city fame.'

'For all the wrong reasons,' he insisted. 'It should never have been allowed in the first place. It's a total disgrace.'

Faye was taken aback by his narrow-minded prejudice. 'Liam wouldn't agree with you. He's been a naturist nearly all his life. I guess he got it from his aunt.'

Wright did not give a damn what her boyfriend thought. He had already formed his own mental picture of him. 'Instead of lying around naked on the beach all day, he should go and get a job.'

'He's got one already,' she put him right. 'He's a ghostwriter. When he first told me about it, I thought he wrote ghost stories. He actually writes books and articles for other people to publish under their own names.'

At this, he puffed out his cheeks. 'Good God woman. Give me some credit. I do know what a ghostwriter is. More to the point, does he make any money out of it?'

She wondered if it was any of the doctor's business but told him anyway. 'Liam's aunt is very wealthy and owns a specialist agency. She gives him ghostwriting work from time to time, but also a very generous monthly allowance. He's her only nephew after all.'

Muttering something under his breath, the doctor rubbed his hands together. 'Thank you, Ms King. You've given me some useful information. More than enough for one day.'

Faye was deeply disappointed. He was ending her session. 'We can't just leave it here. Nearly everything you've asked me about had nothing to do with my panic attacks. I need you to help me. Isn't there something you can prescribe?'

He raised his eyebrows. 'If you're talking about drugs, I don't consider your symptoms to be serious enough. There are medications, but most have side effects, or can be addictive. It's much better for you to try and cure yourself naturally. You did the right thing in coming to see me today. It's extremely helpful to talk through your problems with someone you can trust.'

Of all the codswallop he spoke, Faye considered this to be the most stupid. She had no faith in him at all. As far as she was concerned, the appointment had been a complete waste of time.

Oblivious to her feelings, he had more advice. 'Make sure you stick to a healthy diet. Exercise and try to relax more. You also need to cut back on the caffeine and get more sleep.'

Was this really the root of her problem? Was this the best he could do? 'You've suggested all these things before but none of them have worked.'

'Then you haven't been trying hard enough,' he hypothesised. 'There's one more thing of importance. You and your boyfriend must completely change your lifestyle. Stop all this naturist nonsense and keep your clothes on. If you don't, you're going to end up in real trouble.'

He pointed towards the door. 'I'm sure you can see yourself out Ms King.'

Faye had no option than to leave. Her eyes prickling as tears formed, she was so disheartened. His unethical manner and inappropriate questions had been appalling. It was as if he did not want to help her at all.

Liam had waited outside, whilst she was in with Dr Wright. He had taken the opportunity to phone Jason.

'I'm sorry you couldn't contact me yesterday until late,' his friend apologised. 'My mobile was turned off. We were busy initiating some new members of the Order.'

Not knowing this, Liam had tried several times to get in touch, to tell him about what had happened at the health spa. It had been nearly midnight before they had talked.

'It was no problem,' Liam assured him. 'I just wanted you to know about it as soon as possible. Have you come up with any explanations yet?'

'Let's meet for a drink tomorrow lunchtime and discuss it then?' Jason suggested.

'Good idea,' he agreed. 'Let's say 12 noon at the Fortune of War. Bring Scarlet with you. Seeing her again will do Faye some good.'

'Will do,' Jason promised. 'Where's your lovely girlfriend now?'

He explained she was in with the psychiatrist. 'She doesn't find him a particularly nice man, but we're hoping he will help her.'

Before he rang off, Jason had one other thing to tell Liam. 'When I got home last night, I did some tarot card readings for you both. Quite a few actually, as I had to be certain. I used Aleister Crowley's Thoth deck, as it's the most accurate. Worryingly, the card which came up every time to indicate the final outcome was the same for you and Faye. It was always the Tower.'

Jason did tarot readings professionally and had a reputation for giving exceptionally precise results. Liam on the other hand knew very little about them or how they worked. 'Is the Tower a bad card?'

'The Tower isn't always negative,' his friend expounded. 'It can sometimes, for example, suggest sudden and unexpected changes, which could lead to improvement in the long run. In all your and Faye's readings however, the Tower card was always reversed. In other words, it was upside down.'

Liam thought it a strange coincidence. 'What does this indicate?'

'The interpretation of the cards which preceded the final outcome are of significance too, but I'm gravely concerned.' There was no mistaking the trepidation in his voice. 'Look at what's happened already. First, there was my intuitive warning that you and Faye were under attack. Then, Faye suffered that horrible assault in the health spa. It appears this was only the beginning.'

Hearing this made Liam extremely anxious. 'What did the tarot readings repeatedly predict?'

Jason's reply would send more than a shiver down his spine.

'Danger and destruction; disaster and ruin; injury and sudden death!'

3

The Fortune of War pub was one of their favourites.

On the lower promenade, beneath Brighton's busy King's Road, it had overlooked the pebbly beach since 1882. When the weather was poor, they loved the atmospheric bar inside. It was made up from old boats, cleverly suggesting you were sitting in the hull of an historic warship. On sunnier days, there were plenty of wooden tables with bench-seating outside. This is where they awaited their friends the next day.

When they arrived, they greeted each other warmly.

Liam fetched the drinks from the bar, while the others chose a table. Not wanting their conversation to be overheard, they ensured it was slightly away from other people.

Jason and Liam had become friends after a chance meeting on the naturist beach. This had been soon after the latter had moved to the city.

The shaven-headed 34-year-old occultist was dependable and supportive, always ready to offer guidance and share his beliefs. Extremely spiritual, philosophical and resourceful, his knowledge was immense on all things mystical and supernatural. It was fitting therefore that he earned his living as a tarot card reader and dream interpreter.

Slightly younger, Scarlet had dyed her hair red since Liam and Faye last saw her. She felt the colour better suited her name. She was almost the same height and build as Faye, but retro clothes were her style, hunted down from charity shops. Bubbly, quirky and outgoing, she was always fun to be with. It was probably assets like this, along with her sexy husky voice, which accounted for the number of former relationships she had experienced. They had been with men and women, her days of experimenting ending when she had fallen head over heels in love with Jason.

She was also a very talented jewellery designer. Just a glance at the unique rings on her fingers and the imaginative creations dangling from her earlobes were enough for anyone to appreciate her skills.

How's your business going?' Faye asked, taking a sip of her Prosecco.

'It couldn't be better,' Scarlet enthused. 'Not only have I got my market stall, but I'm selling through several websites now. It takes up most of my time, but at least I'm doing something I enjoy.'

Whilst it was good to see the women chatting, Liam was desperate for Jason to tell him more about the frightening tarot readings. 'Are you sure the cards weren't making a mistake?'

'It's not the cards themselves which predict the future,' Jason explained. 'Their symbolism assists my intuition. The language of symbols is ancient. Dating back thousands of years, they lie at the very base of our subconscious minds. Fate is not predetermined. A divination can only predict the most likely outcome. I passed that on to you yesterday.'

Overhearing this, Faye, was keen to find out what he had said.

Liam had not dared to repeat what Jason had told him the day before.

'Are you going to tell me what the cards revealed?' she asked, having no idea of their frightful significance.

Jason was honest with her and held nothing back. 'The card which kept coming up as the likely outcome for both of you was the Tower. Alarmingly, it was reversed, or upside down. Following on from the cards which preceded it, the likely outcome suggested danger, and destruction; disaster and ruin; injury and sudden death.'

Startled, Faye's jaw dropped. She did not like what she was hearing.

'Such damning consequences are not set in stone,' Jason quickly added, hoping it might suppress her fright. 'Situations can change, but as the old proverb goes, *forewarned is forearmed*. Being aware that something might happen is the best form of preparation. Whilst such tragedies can't be ruled out, we can at least do everything we can to avoid them.'

Scarlet had also been listening carefully. She reached over and took Faye's hand. 'I'm quite sure things won't be so bad.' She tried to sound reassuring. 'Jason's only warning you about possibilities. He'll do everything he can to keep you safe. Just ask some of the other members of the fraternity he belongs to.'

Faye had never been introduced to any of them. It was an extremely secretive organisation, which Jason had not even told Liam much about.

Glancing around, to make sure no one was eavesdropping, Jason decided to be little more open with his friends. 'Our Order is called Fraternitas Mystica Magicka. It incorporates elements of Hermeticism, Alchemy, Freemasonry, Astrology and Aleister Crowley's Thelema. Our lack of any website or social media presence is entirely intentional, as we prefer to remain in the shadows. Aspirants interested in esoteric wisdom, spiritual growth and transformation must seek hard to acquaint themselves with our trusted intermediaries. Our outer symbol is a version of the all-seeing eye.'

He held out his index finger, drawing their attention to the ring he was wearing. 'Amongst other things, this human eye symbolises creativity and self-expression. It also indicates spiritual protection and guards against misfortune.'

They had all noticed the ring before, but only Scarlet had asked about its significance. 'He's got the same eye tattooed on his chest,' she reminded them. 'You've both seen it too, when we've been on the naturist beach.'

Jason's disquiet was for Faye. As he supped his beer, he asked her to describe in her own words what had happened at the health spa.

By the time she had finished doing so, Scarlet was quite upset at hearing the chilling details.

She turned to Jason. 'How do you explain such a freak of a man?'

'I'll come to that in a minute,' he pledged, 'but first I want Faye to tell me how she got on with the psychiatrist yesterday.'

'It was a total waste of time,' she considered. 'Dr Wright was already aware that I suffer from scopophobia, the fear of being stared at. He knows it can bring on panic attacks, but had the audacity to make out it was all my own fault. He didn't believe a single word I told him about the hot tub. Instead, he claimed Liam and I had simply imagined the whole thing.'

'Which would have been impossible,' Liam was keen to add.

'Of course,' Faye agreed, 'but Wright went on about psychiatric disorders I've never even heard of. I think he was trying to confuse me. Most of his questions were highly inappropriate. He was probing for personal information about Liam. The man's arrogant and unprofessional. You'd think he'd had no training at all as a psychiatrist. What's more, he's extremely biased, making it perfectly clear that he hates naturism and wants the beach closed. Rather than helping me, it's as if he wants me to keep on having panic attacks.'

'You could make an official complaint about him,' Jason considered, 'although I'm not sure what good it would do.'

'The biggest problem's going to be when I need to see him again,' Faye predicted.

'Let's hope it's not for some time,' Jason consoled. 'It'll

be of little comfort right now, but I should tell you about another side of scopophobia. The Greeks call it Mati and describe it as the action known as the evil eye.'

He glanced down at his ring. 'Which has nothing to do with this benevolent eye. The evil eye is the malicious stare one person can give another. If the person doing the staring has depraved thoughts and feelings towards someone, they can wish for misfortune to be brought into their lives. Provided they have the power they can make it happen. This is precisely why trained occultists, opposed to any wrongdoing, constantly guard against any unintentional bad thoughts. It's vitally important to prevent a negative one ever materialising by accident.'

'The man in the hot tub was definitely giving me the evil eye,' Faye was convinced.

Jason was trying to work out who or what it had really been. 'It might have looked human, but there's a strong probability that it wasn't. Have any of you ever heard of a thought-form?'

Blank looks confirmed not.

'There's an ancient occult law which states that all our thoughts image themselves in our minds.' He was trying to put across this complex concept as simply as he could. 'Every image continually held in the mind must materialise. There's something known as a servitor. It's an entity created by a magician, or some other person skilled enough. It's like a Tulpa. In Tibetan Buddhism and mysticism it's believed will-power and strength of mind can bring into existence humanoid thought-forms. They're like genies, or to use a modern analogy, robots, which can carry out the wishes of their creator. Such a being can be created in human form by the concentrated power of the mind. It's then sometimes known as a phantom body. It might sound like science fiction, but such entities really can be created by someone, providing they have the know-how. I'm beginning to think it was such a being which attacked you, Faye.'

'How long before you're certain?' Liam asked him hopefully.

Jason needed more time. 'If we're up against someone powerful enough to create something as monstrous as this, then things are a lot worse than I first suspected.'

Finishing his drink, he stood up. 'I've got a fraternity meeting to attend, but I'll ask some of the others if they'd agree. In the meantime, take care and let me know if any more strange things happen,'

Scarlet made to move as well. 'It's been great seeing you again, but like he says, stay safe.'

She had a sudden idea. 'Why don't you do something fun, to take your minds off all this. Go on the pier and have a thrill on the log flume, the roller coaster or the ghost train.'

'What a good idea,' Faye agreed, kissing her on the cheek, 'but I think we'll avoid the ghost train. I've had enough scares already!'

They never did get to the rides.

Halfway down the pier they stopped to look across at the naturist beach in the distance. Being a nice day, there were a good number of people on it.

'That's where we should really be on a lovely day like this,' Liam reckoned, 'enjoying the benefits of the sun.'

'If the weather stays this way,' she vowed, 'we'll go there tomorrow.'

As they walked on, past one of the amusement arcades, they came across a four wheeled gypsy caravan. Painted bright red, it had yellow steps, which led up to a curtained door. On the side of the wagon was a large sign which read *Fortune Teller*. Underneath in smaller lettering it tempted *Let Asteria peer into your future*.

Liam knew of the name Asteria, from a book about Greek mythology, which he had partly ghostwritten. 'She was a Greek goddess of prophecy,' he was able to tell Faye, 'the first daughter of Phoebe the Titan. Her name signifies the ability to see things.' He had no idea how the gypsy wagon fitted in.

'Perhaps we should give her a try,' Faye proposed. 'She might be more positive than Jason's tarot reading.'

Liam hoped so, but did not anticipate much. He agreed anyway, for amusement if nothing else.

Climbing the steps they peeped around the curtain.

A female voice invited them in.

As they did so, their nostrils inhaled the heavy but pleasant smell of incense. In such a confined space it tickled their throats, making them cough.

The burner and a lit candle stood on a small round table, which was draped in a black fringed cloth. Blue curtains, patterned with gold stars, covered the walls and ceiling, whilst mystical new-age music played in the background.

From the candle and spillage of daylight around the entrance, they could make out a youngish blond-haired woman. Her clothing rather spoilt the image inferred by the advertising outside. There was certainly nothing Greek about her white t-shirt. Emblazoned on the front, above a cartoon image of a seagull, was the wording *I Love Brighton*.

Liam wondered why more effort had not been put into looking the part. Even so, he asked how much it would cost for a reading.

'It depends on what you want, love,' came the reply. 'A basic reading is £20, or £30 for the two of you. I can take contactless payment if you don't have cash.'

Reflecting on such convenient technology, compared to that in Ancient Greece, he presented his payment card. 'We'll just have one joint reading please.'

Gesturing for them to sit down on the two padded chairs opposite her, she uncovered a crystal ball.

'The use of these and similar psychic aids dates back to antiquity,' she informed them.

Liam was pleased that at least something was authentic.

'If you have any questions before we begin,' she offered, 'I'll be happy to answer them.'

Faye was inquisitive, having never had such a reading before. 'How does it work?'

'A very good question,' the psychic considered. 'As I gaze into the crystal, I see abstract images. My own intuition interprets them. I then pass on to you what they represent.'

Liam recalled Jason saying something similar about

his use of the tarot. 'Will we be able to see the images in the crystal too?'

The fortune teller signalled not. 'It's very unlikely, unless you have your own natural psychic skills. The ball is more for me to focus on. I go into a trance-like state and use my clairvoyant senses to visualise the images and symbols. What would you like me to foresee? How about your future as a loving couple? I could let you know whether you're likely to get married and have children, own your own house and be well off. That's the kind of thing most people want to know.'

Liam was more specific. 'We need to know if there are any bad things lined up for us.'

Her clients were usually keener to hear the good news, but she agreed. 'That's fine. Just a general reading. One which will cover anything important. We'll get started then. You must both sit quietly whilst I go into a trance. I'm also going to build an energy bond, which will link the three of us. At the same time, you try and think some nice positive thoughts.'

Her eyes closed and she mumbled something to herself. Her shoulders rose and fell, as she took several deep breaths.

She took an even longer one, letting it out ever so slowly. Her hands, palm side down on the table, either side of the crystal ball, were motionless.

Gradually, her head sunk forward, her chin resting on her chest.

Liam and Faye glanced at each other. Was she falling asleep, or going onto a trance? Was all this just part of an act to impress them, or was it for real?

Without warning, her eyes suddenly shot open. They stared directly into the crystal ball. Her face was emotionless. She was concentrating, presumably searching and seeking.

After a while, a look of questioning appeared on her face.

She leant forward, her head much nearer to the ball. It was as if she was checking and then rechecking something.

Shaking her head from side to side, her expression melted into that of unease.

It was followed by suspicion and finally complete disbelief.

Face draining of colour, her mouth gaped open, her body stiffening.

Jerking upright again, her sudden movement suggested alarm and fear.

Frantically waving her hands in the air, it was as if she was trying to wipe away whatever she was seeing.

Body trembling and shaking with terror, she lost complete control.

Leaping to her feet, she grabbed hold of the crystal ball.

Cursing aloud, she flung it to the floor.

From under the table, she snatched a handful of money notes and threw them at Liam. 'I don't want your money! You can have it back in cash. I just want you out of here!'

Liam and Faye were really taken aback. 'What for?' 'Why?' 'Whatever have we done?'

'What did you see?' Liam was desperate to find out.

'Please, tell us.'

'You don't want to know. You really don't,' she insisted. 'No one should be made aware of such horrors.'

Clutching her head in both hands, her fingers desperately rubbed the temples. 'I've got to get what I've been shown out of my mind. If not, I'll go crazy.'

The force with which she pushed them through the doorway, pulled down the curtain rail.

'Go! Now!' she shrieked. 'I've been shown what's going to happen to you. It's horrible. You've got the kiss of death upon you.'

Shocked, Liam and Faye tumbled down the steps.

Steadying themselves, they turned, looking up at the fortune teller.

A *Closed* sign was now hanging beside her at the front of the caravan.

Before disappearing inside, she stared back down at them, her face filled with pity.

'May God save your souls!'

4

The city of Brighton and Hove awoke to a beautiful morning.

Liam and Faye were determined to make the most of the new day, for when the sun shines the heart sings.

As they headed off to the naturist beach, they tried to dismiss yesterday's chilling experience. The fortune teller had scared them no end and her predictions had caused them another restless night. They now regretted having impulsively sought guidance, without even knowing her credentials. She was either an authentic and highly talented psychic, or a dishonourable charlatan. Unwisely, they hoped she was the latter, feeling it might discount her sinister reaction.

'Did you phone Jason about her?' Faye asked. 'He insisted we inform him if anything else happened.'

'Not yet,' Liam admitted. 'I'm unsure what his reaction's likely to be. He'll no doubt think we were foolish.'

'And he'd probably be right,' she anticipated.

Liam wanted nothing to spoil their time on the beach. 'I'll leave it to later.'

They were always pleased to board the Volk's train, which

is supposedly the world's oldest operating electric railway. Running along the seafront on Madeira Drive, the line starts from the Aquarium station just east of the pier and takes passengers to Black Rock. From there it is not far to the Marina and an even closer walk to the famous naturist beach.

Raised banks of pebbles hide the nudists from the train track and road, giving them some privacy from passers-by. Like the other beaches in Brighton, it is of shingle rather than sand. Flip-flops or sandals are the best footwear for crunching over the lumpy grey flint rocks, carried by tides from nearby eroding chalk cliffs.

It was most crowded along the water's edge and so they laid claim to an area further up the beach. The tide was coming in anyway and once settled they did not want to move. Liam unrolled their straw beach mats, which were essential for comfort.

Faye meanwhile unfolded the colourful towels, placing them on top.

Stripping off their clothes and applying coconut scented sunscreen, they surveyed the other beachgoers. There was the regular mix of older seasoned naturists, younger bohemian locals on their day off and a few holidaymakers, some probably first timers. Comprising couples and singles, straight and gay, males as usual outnumbered the women. All seemed happy, enjoying clothes free liberation as nature had originally intended. Some bronzed openly in the sun, others beneath parasols, or beside not really needed windbreaks.

Faye felt comfortable here. No one stared at her,

despite her alluring looks. She closed her eyes, breathed in the briny air and listened to the soothing sounds of the seaside.

A lone seagull flew above her. Its call was soft, hardly more prominent than the sound of the ebb and flow of the gentle sea. Her mind pictured the slightly frothy water, as it rhythmically rolled inland, dissolving amongst the pebbles, shells and strands of seaweed. As her thoughts slowed, so too did all her pent-up stress.

Liam had been watching those brave enough to go for a swim. Early in the season still, all displayed the first shock of cold water against their skin. There was nearly always an initial gasp and often a frantic rubbing of the upper arms. Some took the easy option, retreating prematurely back to their towels. The braver and hardier took the plunge. Decision taken, they waded determinedly into deeper water, before throwing themselves forward. Minutes later, adrenalin released, muscles strengthened, and minds sharpened, they emerged from the sea with a shiver. Most of their smiling faces bore expressions of defiant but satisfying achievement.

Having initially planned to spend only the morning on the beach, by lunchtime they regretted not having brought any food or drink with them.

'Is there anywhere nearby where we can get a sandwich and something to drink?' Faye quizzed Liam.

'There are a couple of cafes near the train's halfway station,' he recalled. 'One's next to the children's playground and the other's at the volleyball courts.'

'Perhaps we should go together,' she suggested.

He pulled on his shorts and stepped into his sandals. 'There's no point in us both getting dressed. You stay here and look after our things. It's not far and so I won't be long.' Checking he had his wallet, he blew her a kiss and set off.

Faye lay back down on her beach towel, closed her eyes and relaxed,

Suddenly, an awful story came to mind. It had been on her smartphone's news app earlier. The report had been about a scorchingly hot beach somewhere in the world. People had begun to smell what they thought was barbecued chicken. It turned out to be coming from an extremely overweight drunkard, who had fallen deeply asleep. With no protection, he was literally cooking to death in the sun.

She screwed up her face at the thought and sitting up, started to apply more sunscreen. Doing so, she wondered whether climate change would make gruesome things like this even more common.

Her thoughts were disturbed by the sight of a middle-aged individual, who was walking towards her. He was dressed in a lounge suit. It was the last thing anyone should wear in the summer, especially on a naturist beach.

As he got closer, she could see he had a camera hanging from his neck. Despite plenty of unoccupied areas on the beach, he came and sat down right beside her.

She immediately felt apprehension. He was disrespecting her personal space.

Her eyes scanned the beach for possible help should

she need it. There was no sight of Liam and everyone else seemed preoccupied.

'I've just come from the Marina,' the stranger claimed, pointing to its massive dark wall. 'Been taking pictures there, of the fishing boats and yachts.'

He lifted the strap over his head as if to hand her the camera. 'I can show you some of them on the screen if you'd like me to.'

'No thank you,' she declined politely. 'I'm waiting for my boyfriend to get back. He's gone to get some food.'

He looked disappointed. 'How about I take a few pictures of you instead then? I've only had the camera for a couple of days and I'm trying it out.'

She promptly picked up Liam's towel and covered the front of her naked body. 'Don't you dare.'

'Please. Just a few,' he pestered. 'You're very pretty.'

She looked around again, even more anxiously, hoping someone might notice that something was wrong. 'Will you go away please? Go and ask someone else.'

Pulling her book from the beach bag, she opened it and pretended to read.

'I don't want to keep the pictures,' he made out, 'but I do need to practise taking them.'

She ignored him, keeping her head buried in the book.

'Just one photo,' he pleaded. 'You can keep the towel around you. I just want to see how the picture comes out. It's not as if I'm going to show it to anyone.'

'How do I know you wouldn't?' she countered.

He had an answer ready. 'I'll give you the memory card from the camera. You'll have the only copy.'

She was desperate to get rid of him, but also gullible. 'If I let you take just one photo, you'll give me the SD card and leave me alone?'

'I promise,' he vowed, quite convincingly.

Standing up, he moved a little further away, to make sure she was in frame.

There was now no possible way she could stop him taking the shot, other than leaping on him in a bid to grab the camera. Instead, she checked the towel was fully hiding her breasts and lower half.

'Smile!' he had the outrageous cheek to encourage, as he pressed the shutter button. 'Not bad,' he judged, looking at the screen. 'There's not much of you in it, except for your face, but it's quite good for my first portrait.'

Faye held out her hand. 'The SD card please.'

A bewildered expression appeared on his face. It was put on. 'So soon? If I remove it from the camera, I won't be able to take any more photos today.'

He pointed in a westerly direction. 'I'm going on the pier next. To take pictures of people getting soaked on the log flume.'

She was flabbergasted. 'You promised you would give me the card.'

'And I will,' he bluffed. 'Once I've finished with it. You give me an address and I'll pop it in the post.'

Faye was furious, with him for his deception and at herself for being so easily conned. The situation seemed to be getting worse by the moment. She just wanted the man to go, but not with a picture showing her face. He might do anything with it. What if he uploaded it onto social media, or used it to generate a pornographic image of her?

He held out a pen and a small piece of paper. 'Just write down where you live. I'll send it first class.'

She was flustered. Her sense of judgement impaired. 'If I give you my address, you'll put the memory card in the post tomorrow?'

'Of course,' he fibbed. 'First thing in the morning. I'll be at the front of the post office queue.'

Common sense seemed to have deserted her. Without thinking of the consequences, she scribbled on the paper and handed it back.

He studied it closely. 'You've only put your address. What about your name?'

'You don't need it.' Foolishly, she was about to disclose even more confidential information. 'My boyfriend and I are the only people living in the flat.'

'The postal service won't deliver it without a name,' the shyster claimed. 'Tell me what it is. I need to write your name and address onto an envelope when I get home.'

This was all too much for her. She had to get rid of him. 'It's Faye King.'

An expression of doubt showed on his face. 'Faking? Are you sure you haven't made it up? If you are faking, you won't get the memory card.'

'It's my real name,' she attested. 'My first name is Faye and my surname's King.'

With a thumbs-up gesture he started to walk away but turned his head. 'Great picture. You should be a model with looks like that.'

Her eyes followed him suspiciously, as he made his

way up the beach. Surprisingly, he headed back towards the Marina, rather than in the direction of the pier.

She could only assume he had a car parked nearby or was getting a bus.

The trickster knew exactly where he was going.

5

When Faye saw Liam returning to the naturist beach, she gave a sigh of relief. How she wished she had gone with him to get the food.

He noticed his towel, which she was still clutching to her body. 'You can't be feeling chilly, on such a nice warm afternoon.'

Handing it back to him served as an answer.

Should she tell him about the photographer or not? It was embarrassing, the way she had handled the situation.

'What did you get for lunch?' she asked, changing the subject.

He unpacked the plastic bag he had been carrying. 'I got us both a sandwich. They're bacon, lettuce and tomato, with mayo on farmhouse bread. There's also water and a couple of beers.'

Kicking off his sandals and stepping out of his shorts he sat down.

A look at her face was enough to tell him something was amiss. 'I thought a BLT sarnie was one of your favourites.'

'You know it is.' Feeling awkward, she resolved to tell him. 'I'm afraid there was a bit of a problem while you were away.'

'Really?' He was concerned to hear it. 'I wasn't gone that long. What happened?'

The way she described it did not help. 'A man came along with a camera. I let him take a picture of me and gave him my name and our address.'

Liam could hardly believe what he was hearing. 'You did what?'

She did her best to explain in slightly more detail how she had been tricked. 'You know how vulnerable I can be.'

He did indeed. It was one of several reasons he felt so protective towards her. Rather than stating his disappointment at her ineptitude, he chose instead to calmly reassure her. 'It's highly unlikely you'll ever be sent the camera's memory card, but let's hope the man was just a pest, a nerd who enjoys disturbing people. Should anything ever happen like that again when you're alone, you must call out for help.'

It had crossed her mind to do so, but she had not wanted to make a fuss. 'I didn't want to disturb everyone, to spoil their peace and quiet.'

'As naturists we have a common bond,' he believed. 'Beaches like this are usually very safe. We look out for each other.'

He handed her a sandwich. 'Let's forget about it and eat.'

Just as he was about to take a bite of his, he noticed something peculiar. There was a slight movement in the bread.

Curious, he lifted the top slice and looked inside. To

his utter disgust, there were lots of filthy maggots. They were crawling all over the filling.

'Don't eat the sandwiches!' he bawled.

It was too late. She was chewing, having already taken a bite.

He could see a maggot dangling between her lips. 'Spit it out!'

Having no idea what he was talking about, she swallowed. 'Is there something wrong with it?'.

Snatching the sandwich from her hand, he flung it onto the pebbles. 'They're full of grubs.'

'What?' She leant forward, peering at the mess.

Seeing them, her head jerked back in disbelief. Dozens of white soft-bodied maggots were wriggling over each other. She could even make out what looked like eyes on the backs of their heads.

Filled with utter revulsion, she watched hideous legless larva slivering from the bread onto the surface of the beach.

Her face crumpled. 'Bloody hell! I've just swallowed a mouthful.'

The realisation made her retch, her stomach churning with nausea.

Gagging, she lost control and vomited.

Fortunately, she managed to turn away from Liam just in time. If not, he would have been covered in the spew.

Neither of them dared look at the sickly mess expelled through her nose and mouth.

They could smell it though. Lingering on the gentle sea breeze was the sharp pungent smell of sour milk, noxious bitterness and musty acidity.

Liam had to swallow hard to stop the contents of his stomach joining hers.

He wisely opened a bottle of water. 'Swill your mouth out with this.'

After doing so, she gasped in deep breaths, trying not to throw up again. Now her body really was shivering, her eyes watering, nose running.

She wiped her face with the corner of her towel. 'I'm so sorry, but why didn't I taste them in my mouth?'

He wisely chose to ignore her question. Having read that the larva of flies sometimes has a mild and pleasant taste, he feared such information might make her vomit again.

'It's the last BLT sandwich I'll ever eat,' she swore aloud.

He was stupefied by what had happened. 'The sandwiches were completely fresh. The lady in the café was lovely. She made them right in front of me. I saw everything she put into them. She washed and then dried the lettuce with kitchen towel. The hygiene and preparation were so good.'

'There were definitely no maggots?' Faye wanted to make sure, wiping her mouth.

'Of course not.' He was at a complete loss as to how they got into the food.

Opening the cans of beer, he passed her one. 'I think we need a drink. Something very peculiar is going on. It doesn't make any sense at all.'

He was right, but it was nothing, compared to what was about to happen.

*   *   *

Slowly, they became aware of the increasing number of seagulls which were gathering around them.

The birds being very common in Brighton, as in many seaside resorts, their presence was nothing out of the ordinary. A solitary one had indeed flown above Faye earlier.

Little had she known it had been on a mission, sent by more dominant birds, to verify her location. Having reported back, whole colonies could now be seen. Rather like squadrons of fighter planes, they approached from every direction.

The earliest on the scene hovered above, awaiting further flocks. Aloft in the updraft, their beating wings stirred the summer air.

Liam and Faye could only watch with growing alarm. Could it be the maggots which were attracting them? Surely not.

Some of the birds lowered their pink-legged landing gear. Gliding effortlessly, they touched down. Their red-spotted, yellow hooked bills resembled lethal daggers. The razor-sharp claws on their webbed and wrinkly feet looked poised to grip their prey, whatever it was. White chests ruffled; feathered silvery-grey, black-tipped wings folded; they waited in an uncanny silence.

Pair after pair of divergent wide angled eyes glared at Liam and Faye menacingly.

She so hated being stared at, even by these creatures.

Until then, neither of them had suffered from ornithophobia, a fear of birds, but that was about to change.

If only they had been able to read the seagulls' thoughts. 'We've come to get you.' 'You've got no chance.' 'You're done for.'

Suddenly, there was a single ear-piercing, screech - *Kreeeeeeeee!*

It was the signal. The call to action.

Embodying the spirit of combined land, sea and air warfare, all hell broke loose.

Seagull after seagull flew into action. *Kree! Kreeee! Kree-kreee!*

High pitched calls came from everywhere at once. *Kreee-kreeee! Kreeee*!

These shrill and aggressive calls were not for food. Stolen fish and chips, burgers and ice creams were off the menu. These *Kree! Kreeee!* screams were of targeted anger towards two human beings.

Kree! Kreee-kreeeeeee! Kreeeeeeee! The ravenous white-headed hunters were after Liam and Faye.

Wheeling, with frenzied dive-bombing, their wings sliced through the air. *Kreee! Kreee-kreeeee!*

Beaks jabbed frantically towards Liam and Faye's faces. The birds were after a special delicacy, their eyes. They were going to peck them out, for the most dominant to feast on. The rest could later share a celebratory banquet of human flesh. *Kreee-kreeee!*

Frantically flailing their arms in the air, Liam and Faye tried in vain to fight them off. No chance at all.

Kreeee! Kree-kreee!

One of them cracked her sunglasses.

Kreeeeeeee! Kree!

Another scored a direct hit on Liam, cutting his forehead. They had drawn blood. *Kreee!*

Faye felt the beginnings of a panic attack but managed to continue thrashing at them. She was determined not to be beaten.

Kreeee! Kree-kreeee! Kreeeee! Kreeeeeeee! The birds had become brutal, violent killers.

Only just in time, the cavalry arrived from across the beach.

Dozens of other naturists ran to Liam and Faye's aid. Initially, they too had only been curious about so many seagulls gathering. Then, realising the mortal danger the two were in, they rushed to their rescue. They were armed with swinging beach towels, open and closed umbrellas, windshield poles and handfuls of pebbles.

Seagulls are a protected species in the UK, but such a law was instantly suspended by the beach goers. This was defence. The flying war machines had to be stopped.

Pebble after pebble became an improvised hand grenade.

As they smashed into birds, feathers flew.

Kreee! Kree-kreee and then only silence from those shot down and grounded.

Like slingshots, whirling beach towels slung seashells as projectiles.

Kreeeeee! Kree-kreeeeee! Splat! More fell. Blood poured from wounds. Feathers turned red.

Umbrellas and poles were hurled like missiles.

Kree! Kree-kreeeee! Whack! Seagull screams filled the air. Eyes dangled from twisted heads.

Thwack! Broken bones jutted from shattered bodies. Dying gulls twitched as they took their last breaths.

Dead Aves, the scientific term, piled higher and higher onto the beach, many with their brains and guts exposed.

Seagulls are not naturally afraid of humans, but with such effective improvised weapons, the balance of power had changed. Being highly intelligent, the birds knew when it was time to retreat.

This was the opportunity for Liam and Faye to escape.

The other naturists yelled at them to run.

Clutching their clothes and beach bags they dashed towards the Black Rock railway station.

Bare footed, as they ran the pebbles cut into their feet. In the panic they never even noticed.

The train was about to depart. They had to board it.

In all the frenzy it had escaped their minds that they were still naked. It was only the surprised faces of people already on the train which first reminded them.

'You'll have to put something on,' the driver demanded.

'Once we're safe,' Liam promised, pointing to the birds. Most carriages were open-sided, but the nearest empty one had windows and a sliding door.

Diving inside, they slammed it shut, partially decapitating a pursuing gull. Lifeless, it fell to the track below.

Feeling a little safer, Liam and Faye slipped on their t-shirts and shorts. He was so proud of her. Sheer resolve had in the end prevented her from having a panic attack.

The train pulled away, but a handful of die-hard beaks still pecked frantically at the windows. It was a wonder the glass did not break.

By the time it reached the halfway station, the gulls seemed to have accepted defeat. There were far fewer of them.

When the Aquarium station came into view, only one of the coastal birds remained. Perched on the carriage roof, even its shrill screeches had ceased.

As they opened the door and stepped off the train, the only sound coming from its beak was the familiar cackling ha-ha-ha-ha call. Usually, this was from excitement over food. Right then, Liam and Faye knew it was laughing at them.

Running across the road, they took shelter in the Volk's nightclub, which opens in the daytime as a bar and restaurant.

'I think we deserve a stiff drink,' Liam instantly decided.

'I'll get them,' Faye insisted. 'You've got to phone Jason and tell him what's happened.'

He got through straight away on his mobile.

Their friend was appalled to hear about the bogus photographer, the maggot-full sandwiches and especially the horrendous seagull attack.

'We're getting nearer to finding who's responsible for all this aggressive abuse,' Jason assured Liam. 'It's likely just one evil person, possibly supported by others. We're almost positive they're operating from somewhere locally, here in Brighton.'

Liam remembered to also tell him about the fortune teller on the pier. His assumption was still that Jason would dismiss the woman as a phoney.

Far from it. 'I know her well,' instead came his response. 'Her real name is Jackie. She might not bother to dress the part, or charge those who consult her much, but she's totally genuine. She's one of the most gifted psychics I've ever met. If she predicted certain things will happen, it's more than likely they will.'

This was the last thing Liam wanted to hear. 'She refused to tell us what she'd seen, insisting that nobody should be aware of such a terrifying future. She gave us our money back and threw us out of her wagon. Her final words were *May God save your souls.*'

'Her reluctance to convey what she had been shown was probably for ethical reasons,' Jason figured. 'I would never give one of my tarot clients, for example, details of when and how they were going to die. It would be immoral. Knowing such detail would haunt them for the rest of their lives. Even if they were sceptical, fear would still constantly gnaw away like a cancer at the back of their minds. This is one of the reasons why fortune telling is still banned in some countries, except for entertainment and amusement. I only ever say what a likely outcome could be.'

'As you did for us,' Liam recalled, 'but she wouldn't even give us that much information.'

'Then my worst fears are confirmed.' The tone of his voice was even more solemn. 'We've got to find the delinquent who's attacking you and fast. I've got members of my fraternity helping with the search. I hate to tell you this, but there's far less time than we thought. The situation is dire!'

6

Liam and Faye had been into the bookshop by the Clock Tower. It was mainly to use the toilet in the café.

They were on their way home when his mobile rang.

'It's Jason. Where are you now?'

'We're in Queen's Road,' Liam told him, 'Going back to the flat.'

'Will you be there this evening?

Liam looked at Faye. 'Are we in tonight?'

She nodded. After everything which had happened on the beach, it was the only place she was going to be.

'Yes,' he informed his friend. 'Do you and Scarlet want to come round for a drink?'

'Great. I've got some good news for you.' He sounded excited about whatever it was. 'We'll be there about eight.'

Liam was impatient. 'Can't you tell me what it's about?'

'I think we've tracked down the bastard who's attacking you,' he shared.

Such great news had to be passed on to Faye. 'He knows who's been causing all the grief.'

She heaved a sigh of relief. 'Ask him who it is.'

Liam fully intended too. 'What's their name?'

'You'll have be patient,' Jason insisted. 'I've got to

double check a few things first, but hopefully it'll be a celebratory drink we'll be having later.'

With such a cliff hanger he rang off.

As they turned into North Road, they were euphoric by Jason's news.

By the time they reached Kensington Gardens, it was as if their problems had already vanished.

Their hearts were lifted anyway, just by being back in the North Laine. This was the Bohemian quarter of the city. Named after a former field, it now referred to four specific streets, all full of interesting independent retailers. In their opinion, it was the best part of Brighton. They loved the atmosphere, which had made it a tourist attraction.

They were fortunate to live in Sydney Street. Just around the corner from Kensington Gardens, they considered it to be the best of all. With its colourful shop fronts, all full of interesting stock, their favourite was one which sold unique silver jewellery. They could not resist peering into the window every time they passed. The family who owned it often gave them a friendly wave. They had even spotted some prosthetic eye rings, almost identical to the one Jason wore. The designer of such treasures was apparently rather famous.

Their small flat, above a shop, was a little further on, past the pub.

As they climbed the stairs, they stopped halfway. Something was wrong.

The front door was ajar, despite them locking it earlier.

Liam peered through the opening, cautiously pushing it slightly to see inside.

'Be careful,' Faye warned, concerned an intruder might still be on the premises.

Liam could not see anyone. The only sound was the ticking of the wall clock.

He took a step forward. His muscles trembled. His heartbeat raced.

He breathed deeply to calm himself.

Within his reach on the wall was his Jian sword. He had bought it from the nearby Chinese store.

Lifting it by its handle from a hanging hook, he pulled off the scabbard. A lethal looking double-edged steel blade was revealed. Although only a replica, it was probably illegal now, due to stringent blade possession laws. At that precise moment, it did not matter. Just holding it gave him more confidence.

Standing in the doorway, sword poised for defence, his eyes searched the living room. The wall-mounted television was still in place, as were all their framed pictures. To the side of the fawn-coloured sofa he could see the media players and speakers.

So busy was he checking all their other possessions, that he accidentally tripped on the yellow floor rug.

Somehow avoiding a fall over the coffee table, he cursed beneath his breath.

Creeping between the two worn leather armchairs, he tiptoed into the kitchen.

Relieved that no one was hiding there, he scrutinised everything carefully, ensuring it was as they had left it.

The fridge's hum sounded noisier than usual, but perhaps it was his imagination. The cooker, microwave, toaster and kettle were all in place. Crockery and cutlery were piled on the draining board, still waiting to be put away. The large wooden oak table and chairs were undisturbed. The fruit bowl was untouched, as were the brown-spotted bananas, apples and large orange it held. In the corner of the room, the rubbish bin was full to the brim. He made a mental note to empty it.

As Liam moved on to the bathroom, there was the sound of movement behind him. Without hesitation, he spun around, his sword arm ready for action.

It was Faye, who flinched at his sudden turn. She had come to give him backing, furnished with the vacuum cleaner's flexi-cord.

'Make sure there's no one lying in wait,' she cautioned.

Finger to his lip, he signalled for her to be quiet and then pushed open the bathroom door.

The sky-blue shower curtain was half pulled. It had been left like that to dry out. Their fluffy red towels still hung drying on the rail. Toothbrushes were in their holder by the sink. Water dripped in the toilet cistern, the sound as regular as a metronome. Its familiarity was somehow comforting.

With only the bedroom to check, it seemed everything was in order.

The wardrobe, cupboard and chest of drawers were all unopened. On the dresser, Faye could see her makeup, nail polish, hairbrush, jewellery box, alarm clock radio and—

They both spotted it at the same time.

It was lying at the centre of their bed. A naked doll.

'Where the hell did that come from?' Liam pondered.

Faye had never seen it before. 'Don't ask me.'

Moving closer, he picked it up. Its body was made of hard pink plastic. The long dark brown hair looked real. The face was quite cute, with a button nose and smiling lips. Only the rather scary staring eyes spoilt its look, opening and closing as the head was tilted. Disturbingly, a hole had been cut into the chest, around the heart area.

As he handed it to her for examination, something rattled inside.

Puzzled, she turned it over and gave it a shake. A small metallic object fell out onto their white duvet cover.

Closer examination showed it to be a bullet. Little did they know that it was the type used in a handgun.

They peered at it in silence for a moment, contemplating its significance.

Faye seemed more concerned about the doll. 'Is it supposed to be modelled on me?'

The thought had already crossed Liam's mind, but he was reluctant to frighten her. 'Why should it be?'

'For a start she's completely nude and her hair is nearly an identical colour to mine.'

Something else was puzzling Liam. 'Someone has got into our flat but doesn't seem to have stolen anything. Instead, they've left behind a child's damaged doll, with a bullet inside. Why? What's the point? Are they trying to tell us something?'

Faye had no more of an idea than him. 'Let's hope it's the only thing they've done.'

Examining the lock on their front door, they found it undamaged. This only confounded the situation. They had no clue as to how the trespasser had gained entry.

'We'll ask Jason and Scarlet what they think, when they come round later this evening,' he suggested.

Liam and Faye sat at the kitchen table eating a combined lunch and dinner. It was a ready meal, cooked in the microwave. They had both undressed, enjoying the relaxation which comes from naked dining.

It had not really been a break-in, as the door had not been forced, or any windows broken. Even so, it had left them feeling unsafe and violated. They considered informing the police, but with nothing stolen and only the appearance of a mysterious doll, they doubted the point. Recalling Jason's original warning that they might not even be safe at home, Liam partly blamed himself. He should have made their home more secure.

Out of the corner of her eye, Faye suddenly spotted something.

A small grey-brown furry animal had jumped out of the rubbish bin.

Realising what it was, she screamed.

In less than a second, she had clambered onto her chair.

Standing aloft, in a high-pitched voice she screeched, 'It's a rat! I've just seen a rat!'

Liam thought she was either fooling, or hallucinating. 'There are no rodents here. We keep the place clean. Admittedly, the bin needs emptying, but—'

She interrupted him. 'That's where it leapt from.'

Still unconvinced, he glanced at the receptacle.

He did a double take, for at that very moment another rodent's head appeared amongst the rubbish. 'No way! It can't be!'

As they watched on, aghast with disbelief, more and more of the nasty gnawing mammals revealed themselves. Some were only small, probably youngsters. Others seemed massive.

They were witnessing the impossible. There was no way so many rats could emerge from such a small bin.

As the creatures slid down onto the black and white linoleum floor, they darted in every direction. Some ran under the chair Faye was perched on. Others had the nerve to scramble over Liam's feet.

'I'm not having this,' he protested, trying to shake them off. His mind raced for a solution. 'The sword,' he concluded, running to fetch it. As he did so, all he could hear was Faye's primal screams.

Never had she reason to tell him she suffered from *musophobia*, the anxiety disorder brought on by an excessive fear of rats. Dr Wright had told her such a phobia was irrational. She disagreed completely with the stupid man. As far as she was concerned, her paranoia was perfectly justified. Rats' teeth might be small, but they are tough and sharp. They bite through cables and wires, furniture and clothing. Of more concern right now was their ability to chomp on human skin. Just the thought quickened her heartbeat.

Liam re-entered the kitchen. The sharp blade of his

sword uncovered, he started to stab at them. He would not usually harm a fly, let alone any larger living creature. Like on the beach, in this instance he had no choice. At least there had been other naturists to help fight off the seagulls. This time, it was only him and Faye.

Mouths wide open, the rats were daring him to fight back. Throating their sinister long squeaks, they signalled their full rage.

One by one, his wielded weapon penetrated their unguarded flesh and bones. Blood spurted and gushed from their pierced bodies. Tiny tummies regurgitated last meals. Brown and yellow urine ran in pools, the sharp odour of ammonia stinking the kitchen.

Disgusted at such a sight, Faye looked away, sweating and shivering all at once. How she hated these minibeasts. The fleas they carry could pass on lethal diseases. The Great Plague of 1665 was surely proof of that, when thousands of people died.

Liam had now shifted his blows to a chopping action. Each time he swiped the blade down, a rat was sliced in half, its innards spilling out.

Further butchering decapitated tiny heads. Severed, the bloodied balls of fur rolled across the floor.

Trembling and shaking, Faye remembered that the gnawers carry ticks as well.

Her hands brushed frantically at her body, intent on stopping the minuscule parasites from hooking into her. If they succeeded in burying their heads under her skin, they would suck her blood like vampires.

As the rats scurried, their tails dragging behind them,

they shat dark brown and black droppings, the diminutive size of rice grains.

Revolted by the filth, Liam hacked faster with his sword.

The pests squealed in pain, as they lay dying.

With tightness in her chest, Faye glanced at the table. Her stomach churning, she watched as two noxious vermin tucked into what had been their dinner. Such a gross sight made her kick the plates to the floor in anger.

They smashed on impact, scattering pieces of sharp ceramic shrapnel into the piling corpses.

Most of the living rats showed no interest in the wasted food. It was not what they were after. Just like the seagulls, it was something else they sought.

For every rodent Liam killed, ten times more inexplicably emerged from the bin. He had the most lethal weapon but was exceedingly outnumbered by their multitude.

Their aggressive hissing grew louder, as they bit and scratched with increased determination.

Gasping for breath, Faye knew Liam was losing the battle. The vermin were winning. Her head was spinning faster and faster. She began to wobble, her legs so unsteady.

Losing her balance, her fainting body crumpled.

She sank to the floor.

She was done for.

Liam stared on in horror.

The biggest rat of all perched on her twisted body.

Faye was the prey the rats had been after!

7

'Faye? Faye?' Liam hoped that gently calling her name would awaken her.

He deliberately avoided touch. She might mistakenly think it was a rat. 'Faye? Can you hear me? It's Liam.'

Very slowly, her eyes opened. They searched from side to side, taking in her immediate surroundings.

Eventually they focussed on his face. She was relieved by his familiarity but disorientated. What was she doing in bed? How long had she been there? Had something happened?

Realising her confusion, he gave her the answers. 'You had a panic attack. Not a bad one, but you fainted. I carried you from the kitchen and laid you on the bed. I brought you round, but then let you rest. You've been asleep for almost an hour.'

She tried to recall. At first her memory had deserted her, but taking in his mention of the kitchen stirred her mind.

She sprung bolt upright. 'Rats! Where are the rats? Are they still in the kitchen? They were all over me, trying to bite me. Oh my God. It was dreadful!'

Feeling her body start to tremble, he calmed her with a

tender kiss on the forehead. Stroking her arms, he lowered her head back down onto the pillow. 'It's alright. The rats have gone. All of them. Neither of us really got bitten either.'

His words made no sense to her. 'But where have they gone? There were so many of them.'

Liam knew his reply was probably going to confound her even more. 'By the time I returned from the bedroom to the kitchen they had nearly all vanished. The last few were scaling the side of the rubbish bin and disappeared inside. They even took their dead with them. None were left behind.'

She knew where they had come from, but also that there had been hundreds in the end. 'They couldn't have all fitted into such a tiny trashcan. There wouldn't have been enough space.'

He had something even stranger to tell her. 'When I emptied the garbage into the wheelie bin, outside in the street, I had a very careful look. There was not a single rat to be seen.'

She could not understand. 'They were definitely there. They attacked us, but you killed as many as you could with your sword. What about the mess? All their blood, guts, urine and droppings?'

'It's all vanished. Don't ask me how, but it has.' He was as astounded as she was. 'The only thing left on the floor were our two broken plates and food, which I swept up.'

She climbed out of bed. 'I need to check with my own eyes, to prove we're not going crazy.'

'Sorry,' he apologised, 'but there's nothing to see. We

can only hope Jason or Scarlet have more insight into what we've experienced.'

As if on cue, the doorbell rang. Knowing who it was, Liam went to let them in.

Faye would usually never dream of welcoming guests whilst she and Liam were nude. Jason and Scarlet being naturists though, she did not bother to dress. She went instead to the kitchen to open some wine.

With understandable trepidation, she peeped around the door before going in. There were no rats. Everything was just as it should be.

With four glasses and the bottle on a tray, she joined the others in the lounge.

'You two make us feel overdressed,' Jason observed.

'We can quickly fix that,' Scarlet declared.

They soon both had their clothes off as well.'

Faye fetched towels for them to sit on. 'I'm not suggesting you've got dirty bums.'

'I should hope not,' Scarlet teased. 'Had we known it was to be an au naturel drinks party, we'd have brought our own. We did at least bring a bottle of red. We can drink it after yours.'

Wine poured and glasses handed out, they toasted each other.

'And here's to stopping whoever's attacking you,' Scarlet added.

They clinked glasses.

'It's what I've really come to talk to you about,' Jason reminded them.

Liam could hardly wait to hear what he had say but knew he must first update him on what had happened. 'I'm afraid there's been some worrying developments to tell you about. We got home to find the upstairs front door open. Nothing seems to have been taken by whoever got in, but they left us a present. I'll show it to you in a minute. Then, when we sat down to eat in the kitchen, we were attacked by hundreds of rats.'

Scarlet could hardly believe it. 'You've got to be kidding.'

'He's not at all,' Faye insisted. She was rather hoping Liam would spare the detail of her having another of her panic attacks. Embarrassed about suffering from them, Dr Wright had quite wrongly suggested they showed weakness of character.

It was as well their guests had a drink in their hands and not food, as Liam ran through what had occurred in all its gory detail. 'What do you make of that?' he asked, after concluding with the rats' complete disappearance.

Jason's response was swift. 'We can discount the rubbish bin itself. It was probably being used as a kind of portal. Doesn't their sudden appearance and disappearance remind you of something?'

Liam got his drift. 'You're referring to the health spa, to the horrible man in the hot tub. You think that the rats were the same sort of thing. Appearing out of thin air, attacking Faye and then vanishing.'

It was exactly what he meant. 'When we talked about it in the pub, I mentioned thought forms, servitors and tulpas. I explained how someone with the knowledge, will power and incredible skills could create a humanoid, an entity capable of carrying out their commands. It would be even easier for them to bring into existence something in animal form. There's a lot more to it than this, but hopefully you get the drift.'

He turned to Faye. 'I'm sorry to ask you this, but did the rats cause you to have a panic attack, like the man at the spa did?'

She felt her cheeks redden but could understand why he needed to know. 'Yes. It was a much milder attack, but they did.'

'Without wishing to worry you unduly,' Jason went on, 'we must also take into account the seagull attack on the naturist beach.'

'But they were very real birds,' Liam pointed out. 'There's no doubt at all.'

'And they didn't succeed in giving me a full-on panic attack,' Faye was keen to add.

'Perhaps not,' Jason acknowledged, 'but I strongly believe they were meant to. Unfortunately, it seems you, Faye, are the attacker's prime target.'

Liam had been told this might be the case, right back from his friend's very first warning. He was still perplexed to hear it. 'Why her, rather than me?'

'Someone seems to have it in for both of you,' Jason reasoned, 'but especially Faye. The perpetrator must know of your phobias and other weaknesses. You're a very close couple, so by getting at you, they're in a way getting at you both. It's highly likely they've got even worse things lined up. Have you considered the identity of the person who got into your flat? Might it have been the man on the naturist beach, you told me about, who was pretending to be a photographer? After he tricked you into letting him take your photo, didn't you unwittingly give him your name and address?'

Such an obvious possibility had until now skipped their minds.

'He should have been the very first suspect,' Faye realised. 'He was such a creep, as well as a cheat. I was such a fool to tell him where we lived. How could I have been so naïve?'

'Would you recognise him again if ever you saw him,' Scarlet asked.

'Probably,' she supposed. 'I did get a good look at him.'

Jason was pleased to hear it. 'That could come in very useful. I think you'd better now show me what he, or someone else, left for you here in the flat'.

While Liam went off to fetch the doll, Faye opened the bottle of wine their friends had brought along. After refilling the glasses, she opened a packet of chocolate biscuits. She for one was starving, the rats having spoiled their dinner.

'This is what the intruder left on our bed,' Liam said, handing Jason the toy.

He studied it carefully, especially the hole in the chest and then the bullet.

'Her hair is the same colour as yours, Faye,' Scarlet observed, 'but the face is not much of a likeness, and she's not got your figure. You're much prettier.'

She thanked her. 'I haven't got a hole in me either. Well, not where that one is anyway.'

Scarlet laughed, but Jason remained resolute. 'Whilst it's lacking your physical assets, I do think it's supposed to represent you. Its lack of clothes is significant from the naturist angle. The hole and bullet are extremely worrying, but let's first talk about the object itself. Have you heard of a voodoo doll?'

The other three indicated they had.

'Good. You'll know then that they're effigies, typically used to stick pins in.'

'They sell them online and in some shops as novelties,' Scarlet added. 'Personal voodoo dolls made of stuffed cloth. They have various slogans of revenge printed on them. You're supposed to glue a photo of someone you want to harm on the head. They're marketed as being suitable for kids over 14 years of age. I personally think it's a bit naff.'

'It's more than that,' Jason objected. 'It's downright dangerous. Just like giving youngsters Ouija boards. Such things are not toys. If nothing else, they can cause a lot of psychological damage. To go back to the real ones, although they're known as voodoo dolls, they're found worldwide. First, they're made to look like the intended victim and then magically linked to them. That's the most important part of the operation. After that, whatever cruel and nasty things they do to the doll, happens to the victim in real life. They're not always given the doll, but when they are it's to scare them. The attacker can build that fear and use it as a very powerful weapon.'

Faye was looking extremely worried. 'Is there anything we can do to stop this from happening?'

Fortunately, Jason had the answer. 'It's vital you break the link between the assailant and the doll. There are various ways you can do this, but the easiest is to visualise a cord, coming out of the doll's solar plexus. See it extending up into the air. Then, take a sharp knife. You must imagine its blade bursting into flame. You can then use it to cut through the cord, at the point where it comes out of the doll. This must be done in one determined and precise slash. Your mind's eye must see the cord twisting and spinning, flying off into the distance. To make sure it can't return or rejoin, you must destroy the doll.'

'How would she do that?' Liam was keen to know.

Jason was pleased he had used the word *she*. 'The doll must indeed be destroyed by Faye, as she's the intended victim. It must first be purified. You can wash it under running water. After drying it carefully, you must burn it. The entire doll must be eradicated.'

'I'm more likely to burn the flat down,' Faye thought aloud.

'Don't worry,' he assured her. 'We'll go down to the beach with you, to an area which is free from observers. We'd better do it now. You'll need the doll, a knife, a bottle of clean water, a towel and something flammable. Hand sanitiser, or booze with high alcohol content will do, plus paper, wood and matches to start the fire.'

After dressing, they made their way down to the seafront. They chose the naturist beach, as it was less likely to be overlooked, especially at night.

There, while they got everything ready, Jason reminded Faye of exactly what she must do. When she felt able, they began.

After visualising the cord, cutting it with the knife and so on, she lit the fire.

As the doll burned, together they chanted, 'The cord is broken and with it the link. The voodoo doll is destroyed. So mote it be.'

Liam pulled from his pocket the bullet, which had been inside the doll. 'What do we do with this?'

'Faye had to burn the doll, but I can safely destroy the bullet,' Jason offered.

Scarlet had been thinking about its importance. 'What significance does it have.'

'Bullets have many symbolic meanings' he explained. 'Some are positive, others negative. In Buddhist teachings for example, the path to enlightenment involves overcoming obstacles and challenges. A bullet therefore could symbolise the hurdles to be confronted in the search for wisdom and self-realisation. Even when facing a foe, there's the potential for spiritual growth, sometimes through sacrifice. On the other hand, bullets are used in warfare and self-defence. In that scenario they either represent protection, or violence and aggression, power and control. When they're used to harm or kill someone, they signify death. Pins are usually stuck into a voodoo doll. In the one left for you, a bullet was used instead, inserted through the hole made in the chest.'

Faye was scared by this. 'Does it mean I'm going to be

shot in the heart?'

Jason concealed his concern. 'I sincerely hope not, but it's essential you do one thing. Try and forget all about the nasty doll and the bullet it carried. It's easier said than done but you must forget. Should it ever come into your thoughts, even for a second, never let it bring on fear. Instead, simply dismiss it with laughter. Make sure you laugh out loud. It's the simplest and most effective banishing ritual there is.'

Now was the time for Jason to tell them what he had been able to find out about their attacker.

'We've got some of the members of the fraternity to thank for what we've come up with so far. They've learned of a strange Christian cult based here in Brighton. They call themselves the Guardians of Modesty. Their ideas are fanatical. They especially loathe public nudity and consider it a huge sin. These fundamentalists are led by a preacher known as the Reverend. We've tried to find out more about him, but it's been impossible. Not even his followers know his real identity, where he came from, or where he lives.'

'Why would he choose such anonymity?' Liam probed.

'There could be endless reasons,' Jason concluded. 'We don't know whether he's a real Reverend or not. Using the title as a name lets him express his extremist ideas without fear. This might be for personal reasons, or he could have something to hide. There's even the possibility of criminal activity with less threat of detection. Most worrying is the complete control he has over his congregation. This makes him extremely dangerous. When it comes to threatening you, we have no idea of his supernatural powers. Let's hope I find out more tomorrow, when they hold their next meeting. You can be sure of one thing. I'll be there, secretly observing everything this so-called Reverend does and says.'

8

The congregation raised their arms in adoration. 'Hallelujah! Praise the Lord!'

At least forty worshippers had gathered in the small hall, not far from Brighton railway station. Every one of them eagerly awaited their leader's sermon.

The Reverend stepped onto the small rostrum, gesturing for his flock to be seated. No lectern was needed, as he always spoke from memory.

For a moment he remained silent, letting their anticipation mount.

In his late fifties, he was lanky, of pale complexion, grey haired, but balding on top. Dressed in a full-length black robe, he chose not to wear a clerical collar, but from a chain around his neck hung a very large and expensive looking gold crucifix. Highly respected by all present, his authority was unquestioned. A charismatic natural orator, his preachings were always inspirational and motivational. Crucially, his flock believed everything he said.

Knowing he had their full attention he began. 'It never ceases to amaze me. Every time God talks to me, I am filled with humility and overwhelming gratitude.'

'Praise be to God!' the assembled ones chanted.

'His son, our Lord Jesus Christ, is also in continual conversation with me. I am truly blessed.'

'Hallelujah! Praise the Lord!' The refrain echoed around the hall.

'I was ordained by God to pass on his commands to each and every one of you.'

'Praise be to God!' they cried out in perfect harmony.

He signalled silence. Enthusiasm was one thing, but their interruptions were becoming tedious.

'I was instructed to remind you what our Holy Bible says in Proverbs 7:10 - *The woman approached him, seductively dressed and sly of heart.* As the Guardians of Modesty, the name given to our sacred doctrine, we are obliged to stop such evils. In their ignorance, some other Christian Churches quite wrongly describe us as an eccentric cult. How far from the truth. We are the only ones truly carrying out God's commands. Society has strayed from traditional Christian values, leading to moral decadence. Our central conviction is to rightly preserve modesty in all aspects of life. It is essential for the avoidance of sin.'

'Hallelujah! Praise the Lord.' The phrase had become the cult's mantra.

The Reverend again asked for quietness. Supressing their responses momentarily would intensify them later when he commanded. His use of body language being perfect, every gesture he made emphasised what he was saying.

'So, in Proverbs, the woman approached the man. It was not the other way around. No. The woman was the temptress. She was dressed seductively. What could be more seductive than total nudity?'

The Reverend was extremely good at twisting words and meaning to suit his needs. 'She was sly of heart, in other words cunning and crafty. Her intention was to lead the male astray. She was inviting him, as a prostitute would, to indulge in immoral sexual activity, rather than spiritual devotion to God.'

He was speaking with his usual confidence, decisiveness, fearlessness and vision. He would pause at the right moment to let them consider his words.

'Contrast this to the way you all dress. Look around, at each other.'

He waited patiently whilst they did so.

'What do you see? Modesty! Why is this? It is to reflect your reverence for God and crucially to avoid any temptation. All you men are so smart in your lounge suits. Even on less formal occasions, you still wear trousers and long-sleeved shirts, always buttoned up at the front. As for you women, you always ensure your dresses are ankle-length, with high necklines and sleeves to the wrists. Full body coverings are also rightly donned should you ever go swimming. Never forget that the human body is a sacred temple. It is reason enough for us to detest public nudity, whether it is named naturism, nudism or anything else. It's completely incompatible to our central principle of modesty.'

The congregation signalled agreement.

'This is why we must rid the world of public nudity. I'm doing everything I can to make this happen. I have the full power of God and his beloved son Jesus Christ to assist me. Through their divine intervention, naturists will be punished directly. Natural disasters will soon befall their communities. God wants your help too. Every one of you. You must spread our message to all communities. In return, you will be guaranteed a place in Heaven. The good Lord promises you this. Organise and attend rallies denouncing public nudity. Hand out anti-naturist flyers. Lobby politicians and the police to criminalise nudist activities. New stringent laws need to be introduced against public nudity. God's work will only be completed when naked sunbathing and swimming, nude beaches, naturist clubs and resorts, saunas, naked walks and bike rides are all outlawed. The world must be rid of them forever. Hallelujah! Praise the Lord!'

'Hallelujah! Praise the Lord!' the Guardians parroted, rising to their feet. 'Praise be to God!

The Reverend's hold over them was hypnotic, but he had a few more words to add. He asked them to be seated again.

'In playing your very own part in God's work, you have a duty to report any public naturist gatherings to the authorities. Make plain that they are causing you harassment, alarm and distress. They will indeed be, because of your holy beliefs. Whenever possible, make accusations of indecent exposure and sexual offences. It matters not if your claim is false. God will never punish you for a tiny fib, for you are doing his will. Protest outside nudist clubs and resorts. You must especially shame and intimidate the naturist harlots and whores. Label them as being immoral and deviant, so they are shunned. By doing so, you will discourage the innocent and unwary from ever embracing what they call social nudity. Your actions will save them from Hell. You will become their personal saviours, just as the good Lord is ours!'

'Hallelujah! Praise the Lord!' 'Praise be to God!' 'Hallelujah! Praise the Lord!' 'Praise be to God!'

He let them indulge themselves for a while this time, before loudly clapping his hands. 'God is so proud of you. We will now sing Psalm 23 - *The Lord Is My Shepherd.*'

For very personal reasons, he particularly liked the second line, *I Shall Not Want.* 'During this we will have the collection. Our Lord Jesus Christ asks that you give generously. It is important you remember that your contributions during collections are additional to the monthly ten percent tithe you pay the Church. God bless you. Your reservation for a place in Heaven is confirmed!'

9

Liam was completely taken aback by Faye's suggestion during breakfast.

Despite hating being stared at, she had just proposed they take part in the Brighton Naked Bike Ride.

'It's not as if there would only be the two of us,' she reasoned. 'I'm told up to a thousand people might participate.'

He was still extremely sceptical. 'But you've always been rather shy about being nude in public, except when you're with me, or our friends.'

She seemed to think it would increase her self-confidence. 'It's something I've got to do, if I'm going to stop having panic attacks. Dr Wright's been a complete waste of time and so I've got to do it myself.'

Liam was not at all sure the bike ride would help. 'Whilst it could perhaps be beneficial, it could just as easily have the opposite effect.' He knew it had taken place in Brighton for quite a few years, but it had never really appealed to him. 'I doubt Jason and Scarlet will be going.'

'They couldn't even if they wanted to,' Faye knew. 'He's got a meeting and she's busy with her jewellery stall tomorrow. I know the ride's not really a naturist event, although it does celebrate the human body. Not everyone will be completely naked but will be encouraged to be as nude as they dare.'

'Which is just as well,' he wisecracked. 'If they were all fully dressed, it wouldn't be a naked bike ride.' He was aware that there were now similar rides in more than fifty cities around the world, all acclaiming the bicycle as a means of transport. 'The main idea is to raise awareness of vulnerable cyclists on traffic-congested roads and bring attention to fossil-fuelled climate change.'

She had already learnt this online. 'Exactly. They're all good causes you would support. It'll be fun. There's supposed to be a great party atmosphere, with painted bodies, fancy dress, lots of colourful flags, waving banners and good music. Everyone gathers at Preston Park and some people decorate their bikes.'

He was still not convinced. 'How long's the actual ride?'

She had carefully researched the facts before broaching the subject. 'About seven miles, all around the city. It starts at 2pm and ends up on the naturist beach for a swim and afterparty.'

'Let's hope the weather stays dry then.' There was one major obstacle he felt she might have forgotten about. 'Perhaps it's slipped your mind, but neither of us have a bike.'

She had got this covered too. 'There's plenty of bicycle shops here in Brighton, or we can hire a Beryl bike. It's a share scheme named after Beryl Burton, the English racing champion. With hundreds of hubs across the city, there's even electric ones if you're feeling lazy.'

He had to admire her keenness, especially after everything she had been through. Her resolve was extraordinary. He only hoped it might lift her spirits and put the attacks to the back of her mind.

'Alright,' he finally agreed. 'We'll do it. You make the arrangements. I'll cover the costs.'

Filled with excitement, the reward she bestowed on him was far from expected.

With all the stress she had been subjected to, their physical love life had suffered. Understanding how anxiety and panic attacks can impair sexual desire and response, he had avoided putting any pressure on her. Now though, the seductive look she gave meant only one thing. She wanted him to make love to her.

Without uttering a single word, she dragged him by the arm through to the bedroom and onto the mattress. Being nude already, they had no clothes to remove. Their mindset had changed, however. No longer was their nakedness for the naturalness of nudism, but sexual intrigue and fulfilment.

Liam had always been the dominant one, the encourager of their lovemaking. It was how they both liked it. This time was different. She was doing the urging, in gratitude for all the love and support he continually bestowed.

Eyes closing, their lips met in a scorching kiss.

Initial cuddling quickly escalated into needy foreplay.

With firm but gentle caresses, his hands explored her

sensitive skin.

Simultaneously, her fingertips trailed his body seductively.

Each eagerly pleasuring the other's erogenous zones, initiated shivers of sensual delight.

Their entire tingling bodies had become erotic playgrounds; earlobes, cheeks, necks, chests, breasts, nipples, buttocks, inner thighs and new ones just discovered. All were cravingly explored and stimulated.

Such heavenly rapture was in silence, except for the orchestration of deep throaty groans of bliss and breathy sighs of joy.

Anticipation building, their most intimate and amorous parts were treated. The stimulation of his manhood and her sacred rose aroused what nature had so cleverly designed.

Pent-up desire quickly blossomed into full scale lust. With him on top, her legs opened further in urgent desire.

Without further delay, her hand guided him carefully inside her sacred centre of love; the sanctified chapel through which all of humanity is conceived and given birth to.

That special moment. The sharp drawing-in of breath and then stillness, treasuring their celestial union.

Movement, slow and measured to commence.

His thrusts, gaining momentum, her hips in complete chorus.

The pace of breathing changing.

Heartbeats racing, as plunges deepen.

Blood pressures rising. Bodies shuddering. Muscles

contracting. Waves of tingling.

Finally, the avalanche of exhilarating, out of this world excitement.

Mind blanking orgasmic release. Ejaculation.

Rapture. Absolute euphoria. Paradise pulsing through their bodies.

And then tranquillity. Sedateness. Composure.

In the warm fuzzy afterglow, came whispered words of precious shared love and devotion.

Together, as one, they had experienced the ultimate discernment of spirituality.

Real divinity had been discovered, the one and only true religion.

The next day, they arrived at Preston Park just after midday. Not having ridden bicycles for some time, their legs were rather achy and their backsides saddle-sore.

Even this did not dampen Faye's zeal. 'Just think of all the exercise we're getting,'

Like the others, they got undressed. He had wisely brought his backpack to put their clothes in.

Wearing just their sandals, they applied suntan lotion and checked out their fellow cyclists.

Everything was extremely well organised. As an increasing number of participants made their appearance, the crowd's exhilaration was overwhelming. There were more men than women present, but Faye was pleased to see a greater proportion of females than she had expected.

Some were busy with body paint, creating imaginative patterns and effects. Others wrote colourful slogans on each other's skin. Banners and flags were being tied and strapped to bikes. Some had trailers attached, which carried loudspeakers. Pop music boomed and people danced.

The wiser ones queued to use the portable toilets, knowing how long the ride was. Everyone chatted, catching up with old friends, along with acquaintances, some having presumably met at previous rides.

The friendly stewards, dressed in bright yellow jackets, made every effort to smile. Uniformed police officers looked on approvingly. Everyone was good natured, behaving themselves and anticipating the fun to come.

Eventually a huge cheer went up. Bells ringing and horns hooting, the ready-to-go cyclists began to peddle. Brighton's Naked Bike Ride had begun.

Leaving Preston Park, they made their way down towards the Level, an urban park surrounded by elm trees. Quite a few spectators lined the pavements, waving and applauding encouragement.

As the bikes headed south towards the city centre's Old Steine, the number of people watching increased.

Liam was not sure how Faye would react to so many onlookers. Mindful of the number of photographs being taken, they made sure they were surrounded by other riders.

Reaching Brighton Pier, they turned right, riding along the seafront towards Hove, the other part of the city. Here, everyone took a break on the lush green grass of the Lawns, easing their legs and rehydrating with bottled water.

* * *

The second half of the ride routed them through Hove and back into Brighton. Passing the many houses, shops and cafes in Church Road and Western Road, they soon reached the iconic Clock Tower.

Turning right took the riders back along the seafront, then northwards towards the Royal Pavilion. It was the former seaside retreat of the Prince of Wales, later to become King George IV.

Disaster! When they got to their home area of North Laine they ran into trouble. Liam got a puncture and had to dismount.

They pulled over to the side of the road, so as not to hold up the other riders. Liam had no puncture repair kit. There would not have been enough time to use one anyway. Reluctantly, he realised he had to drop out of the ride.

Whilst feeling sorry for him, Faye surprised him yet again by declaring she was going to continue. 'I've said all along that I'm doing this to improve my confidence.'

'But it's going to be even more testing for you without me,' he warned.

Her mind was made up. 'I'll be alright. It's not as if I'm going to be alone. There'll be all the other riders.'

He was really concerned about how she was going to cope. An even greater number of spectators might be watching the latter part of the ride. She had been through so much in the last few days.

'If you really insist,' he reluctantly accepted. 'I'll find a hub to return my bike to and get a replacement. By then, the ride will be over, but I'll meet you on the naturist beach, by the boundary sign.'

'You'd better,' she stressed. 'You've got my clothes and phone in your bag.'

He took her mobile from his bag. 'At least take this, just in case you have any problems.'

She drew his attention to her naked body. 'And where do you suggest I keep it? I need to hold on tight to the handlebars. I won't be able to do it with a phone in my hand.'

He held out his backpack. 'Well take this then. I only need my shorts to get to the bike hub.'

She declined his offer. 'I really won't need the phone or my clothes until after we leave the beach. You look after everything until you come and join me.'

Her tenacity brought him no comfort at all, but he gave her a kiss. 'If you're going to continue, you'd better get on with it, or you'll be left behind. I'll join you as quickly as I can.' As he started pushing his bike away, he so wished he had insisted on her at least taking his bag.

Faye remounted. Taking a deep breath, she joined what were now the riders at the rear.

It seemed strange at first, not to have Liam by her side. She tried to ignore all the spectators who were cheering and applauding. Instead, she was concentrating all her efforts on completing the ride.

They were half-way along St James Street, which runs north of, but parallel to the busy Marine Parade, when catastrophe occurred.

Suddenly, out of nowhere, a giant of a man appeared right in front of her.

She clasped the brake levers tight, her shoes grating against the road, as she desperately tried to stop.

Her front wheel slammed into his legs, bringing her to an abrupt halt.

Faye recognised the man immediately. His face was permanently fixed in her memory.

It was the horrifying fiend from the hot tub!

The bald brute was dressed exactly as he had been the last time she had seen him. He was wearing the buttoned up sleeved shirt and dark trousers. His eyes still bulged, just as they had when he had stared unwaveringly into hers.

Just the sight of him made her shake with fear.

She tried but failed to avert her eyes.

Grabbing her bike by the handlebars, the monstrosity threw it sideways onto the ground. She went with it, flat onto the tarmac.

Looking up, she saw him for just a split second. His face was expressionless.

Then he disappeared into thin air, exactly as he had at the health spa.

Several of the riders, who had swerved to avoid her, rushed over and helped her up. Are you alright?' 'What happened?' they all asked at the same time. 'Are you hurt?

She was dazed and her wrist ached, from where her hand had broken her fall. Too embarrassed to admit it, she told them she was fine.

'Did you see him,' she questioned urgently. 'You must

have. It was him!'

There was an exchange of blank faces. 'Who?' came their reply.

'The huge man,' she explained. 'He appeared right in front of me, knocking me off the bike.'

The only response she received were more baffled looks and shrugging shoulders.

How on earth had no one else seen him? He had been right there, in the middle of the road.

'Are you absolutely sure you didn't?' she pressed again.

'All I saw was you falling off your bike,' one of them confirmed. The rest agreed.

She was so disappointed. It would have made all the difference.

One of the stewards intervened. 'You all need to move on, to re-join the rest in the ride.'

'Yes, you make a move,' she insisted to those who had come to her aid. 'Thanks for your help, but I'm okay. I'll join you in a moment.'

As they rode away, she pulled her bike over to the side of the road and sat down on the pavement. Her right leg was slightly grazed, but there was no blood.

Stragglers at the very back of the ride passed her by.

The police van bringing up the rear, came to a halt when they saw her.

An officer leaned from the window. 'Are you taking a rest?'

'Kind of,' she lied to save face. 'I'll catch up with everyone in a moment. There's no need to worry.'

'As long as you ride with everyone again,' he insisted.

'If not, you must put some clothes on. You can only be nude whilst you're in the ride, or on the naturist beach. It would never do to have you here in town all by yourself and in just your birthday suit.'

He drove on, muttering something to the officer sitting beside him.

Faye got up, righted the bike and remounted. It was only when she tried to peddle that she found the front wheel would not turn. It was locked solid, the brake jammed tight against the front wheel.

Trying to pull the brake lever apart made no difference. Neither did tugging at the rim brake with her fingers. It was stuck fast, making the bike unrideable.

She lay it down again and sat beside it, her head in her hands. What on earth was she to do?

The frightening appearance of the weirdo from the hot tub had really upset her. She could not rid his image from her mind. Jason had concluded that it was a thought-form or something. Whatever it was, it had thrown her from her bike and scared her stiff.

She looked down the road. By now the bike ride had long disappeared into the distance. A few people entering the street were not even aware it had taken place.

All these fully dressed people saw was a completely naked young woman, sitting on the pavement.

10

Faye had never felt so awkward, so exposed and vulnerable. To be the only one naked among so many fully dressed people was a living nightmare.

In childhood and as a teenager living with her parents, she had been conditioned to conform to social norms. Wearing clothes in public was a definite expectation. Instead, now a few years older, here she was, displaying her nude body to every passer-by.

Her head bowed, she closed her eyes, trying to pretend there was no one else around.

It failed to work. There were still the sounds of people going about their business, of vehicles passing by and the smell of exhaust fumes.

Liam had introduced her to naturism, but this was something else. In the bike ride she had been one of hundreds. Here, she was the only one naked.

People were surely judging her and questioning her motivation for such anti-social behaviour.

One certainly was.

'You're a filthy bitch!' This initial insult came from of an elderly woman. 'You should be ashamed, showing off your private bits.'

Without even looking up, Faye knew the spiteful criticism was aimed solely at her. She cringed, her face reddening further.

Peeping through one eye, her fear was confirmed. Her self-esteem plummeted.

The pensioner had a look of disgust on her face. She was keeping her distance, skirting around Faye, her back pressed up against a shop window. She might just as easily have been avoiding a pile of dog excrement on the pavement.

Such a cruel confrontation made Faye feel as dirty. 'I was in the naked bike ride,' she tried to explain. 'The front wheel of my bike got jammed.'

The sour-faced senior was not interested in the least. Scoffing in repugnance, she threw her head back and hurried on.

Completely shocked, Faye gritted her teeth in frustration.

Crossing an arm across her breasts, she covered her womanhood with the other hand. It had little effect.

Upon sighting her, a mother approaching from behind protectively picked up her child.

'Mummy, why's that girl not wearing anything?' the minor questioned innocently.

'She's probably a pervert,' came the stern reply. 'Take your eyes off her. Look the other way.'

'Quite right,' someone else agreed. 'The tart should think of the children before stripping off like that in the street.'

Never had Faye suffered such public humiliation. The

ongoing verbal abuse breaking her heart, she burst into tears.

Two well-dressed middle-aged men came from the other direction. Seeing her, they stopped for a moment and faced one another, analysing the situation.

'Psychiatric problems I should imagine,' diagnosed one.

'Definitely,' agreed the other. 'Escaped from the mental hospital no doubt.'

Faye was completely unprepared for such ridicule. 'I'm not mad,' she tried to reassure them. 'I was in the naked bike ride, but a man threw me to ground before disappearing. It was the same one as in the hot tub at the—'

'You're disgusting,' someone else claimed. 'You should be locked up. Is no one going to call the police?'

Hoping so much that someone would do just that, Faye's chin was trembling, her mouth dry, her heart pounding faster.

'You should leave her alone,' a younger and more understanding woman insisted. 'She's most likely just a naturist. There were lots of them riding bikes around the town earlier. It happens once a year. They're not doing any harm. What's wrong with the human body anyway?'

Faye breathed a sigh of relief. Someone was supporting her, giving reason for her lack of clothing. She felt like leaping up and throwing her arms around them in thanks. Unfortunately, the nicer person was in the minority.

'They should stay on that bloody nudist beach,' an old bigot declared. 'The Council should keep all the degenerates there. Round them up and fence them in.'

Faye was appalled by such narrow-minded fanatical prejudice. She had thought people were by now far more accepting of naturism. Brighton was supposed to be an open-minded, friendly and tolerant community. Was it so unusual to spot a naked person on the street? Surely it must happen quite often, especially on a booze-fuelled Saturday night. With all the hen and stag parties in the city at weekends, it was inevitable. This was mid-afternoon however, she reminded herself, and in broad daylight.

Her heart sank further as three men in their early twenties came out of the betting shop. By the look of them, it was obvious they had been drinking earlier.

Seeing her, they crossed the road with gusto to get a closer look.

'Corr! She's a bit of alright!' the first of them told his mates.

'Nice pair of tits,' agreed the second.

She quickly clasped her breasts with both hands, attempting to cover them. It was not the wisest of moves, being misconstrued as self-fondling.

'I bet she's a good shag,' the other one dared to presume.

Hardly believing what she was hearing, she pressed her knees firmly together. 'How dare you say such insulting and sexist things. Clear off and leave me alone!' She only hoped her words would not escalate the situation.

'Not until I've taken a photo,' one told her, pointing his mobile phone.

Recalling what had happened with the photographer on the beach, her mind scrambled thoughts on how to diffuse her plight.

Using her hair to hide her face, she rolled onto her stomach, to hide her femininity. It was another big mistake.

'Nice arse too!' all three observed.

Struggling with embarrassment, her mind was awash with so many emotions at once. Despair. Defencelessness. Self-pity. Remorse. Regret. How stupid she had been for wanting to take part in the bike ride in the first place. How naïve she had been. With everything else that had happened recently, something had to go wrong. Of course it did. The other riders must have had lots of fun, but not her. Why had she been stupid enough to carry on without Liam? Now, here she was, being accosted by three immature yobs.

She was fed up, attempting to explain to people what had happened, but tried again. 'I was in the naked bike ride with my boyfriend, but he got a puncture.'

'I bet he gets something far more noticeable,' the tallest one supposed, 'when looking at such a sexy body.'

She was unsure if his inappropriate reference to her figure was intended as a compliment or not.

Tired of such childish insults and suggestions, she stood up and faced them squarely 'If one of you was man enough, you'd offer me your jacket to cover myself with.'

'And spoil the entertainment?' came the reply. 'You're giving us an even better view now.'

He snapped another photograph.

A car passed, forcing the men to move off the road.

The driver pulled up and wound his window down. 'Good for you, girl,' he shouted. 'If you've got it, flaunt it, as they say. Power to the people!'

The vehicle behind him was beeping its horn, thankfully forcing him to move on.

Then she saw them.

A whole crowd of football supporters were coming down the road.

'We are Brighton!' they chanted. 'Seagulls!' 'Good Ol Sussex by the Sea!' 'Seagulls!'

Faye knew there was no reason at all why they should be unpleasant to her. It was their sheer number which scared her.

Desperately, she looked around for somewhere to hide.

Seeing the open door of a nearby café, she dashed for it.

Her way was blocked by one of the staff. 'You're not coming in here, not stark naked. There's hygiene to consider.'

Such a comment might have been ridiculous, but it really hurt her, deep inside. 'I'm not dirty,' she wailed in frustration. 'I'm perfectly clean. 'Please, I just need help.'

'You're telling me you do,' he agreed, 'from a psychiatrist.'

Faye stood on the pavement. She had nowhere to go, no place to run.

She had become an outcast, a pariah, an undesirable. It was too much for her to take. Paranoia had been building all the while. Nausea. Hyperventilation. Her entire body trembled, limbs shaking.

As her head spun faster and faster, she covered her eyes, but it made the dizziness worse.

She knew what was coming. It had happened so many times before. She was going to faint.

Her legs gave way.

She collapsed into a heap.

People still noticed her. Some walked around her. Others had to step over her. All were far too busy to get involved.

Instead, most assumed she was just another drunken down-and-out, or maybe a junkie, high from a fix.

11

'So, Ms King,' Dr Wright began, 'you've had another of your panic attacks.'

Faye could remember being greeted with precisely the same words when she last saw him. His bedside manner had obviously not improved. If it had, he would have come up with a friendlier welcome.

Her face flushed, just as it always did when her weaknesses were being discussed.

'What brought it on this time then?' the psychiatrist asked. 'Don't tell me you've been in another hot tub.'

She knew he would find whatever she said laughable. Perhaps if she came up with something incredibly outrageous, he might just be fooled into believing her for once. Although tempted to tell him she had been abducted by aliens, in a UFO disguised as a flying rainforest, she stuck to the truth. 'I was in the naked bike ride.'

Rolling his eyes, he raised them to the ceiling. Such body language was intentional.

She had no idea whether his disrespectful gesture was through mockery, disbelief or lack of interest.

It turned out to be exasperation. 'Just in case you've forgotten, you suffer from scopophobia, the fear of being stared at.'

Faye so wished he would speak a little quieter. She did not want the whole place to hear what he was saying.

'So, what did you decide to do?' If anything, he was even louder. 'Stark naked, you rode a bicycle around Brighton and Hove.'

'When you put it that way,' she reluctantly had to agree, 'it probably wasn't such a good idea, but I was trying to build up my confidence. It was going fine until my boyfriend got a puncture. I tried to carry on without him, but then the horrible man from the hot tub appeared out of nowhere. He was right in the middle of the road, blocking my way. He threw me and my bike to the ground.'

The psychiatrist swivelled his chair away from her, so that he could rest his arms on his executive desk.

'What happened next?' he delved, holding his head in his hands.

'The brute disappeared into thin air,' she divulged, 'just like in the health spa.'

He half-turned back towards her. 'Did everyone else see all this?'

'Unfortunately, not,' she regretted. 'It all happened so quickly. In the blink of an eye. Having damaged my bike, I couldn't continue. I was left alone, sitting on the pavement.'

'Completely nude I presume?' There was emphasis on the second word.

It did not go unnoticed. 'Yes, I was starkers. Liam had all my clothes with him and my phone. I had nothing on me at all.'

His rotating left hand gestured for her to continue. 'What happened next?'

'Some of the people in the street were so nasty to me,' Faye recalled. 'They said some very unpleasant and insulting things. I felt a panic attack coming on and fainted. I don't know how long I was left lying there, but eventually someone called the police. They gave me first-aid and took me home. A nice policewoman was good enough to stay with me until they found Liam. He was on the naturist beach, looking for me. They brought him back to the flat, telling him I should see my doctor this morning. The surgery arranged the appointment with you and so here I am.'

She paused, aware of the repetitive sound of his unskilled typing.

Peering closer, she could see he was only using his forefingers to drum at the laptop's keyboard. It was a wonder he did not break it, with his heavy-handed thumps.

'It all backfired really,' she went on. 'If Liam hadn't got the puncture and if the hot tub man hadn't knocked me off the bike, everything would have been all right.'

Whilst she was about it, she thought it best to update him on a few other things. 'Life's been awful since I last saw you. What with terrifying tarot and crystal ball readings, maggot-filled sandwiches and the ambush by schizoid seagulls. Then there was our flat being broken into and the chilling voodoo doll which we later had to burn.'

His visible lack of surprise at what she had told him was encouraging, or so she thought.

'Was that it?' he enquired, as if she had just described

the average person's typical day.

'Basically,' she concluded, 'except for the rats. Hundreds emerged out of our kitchen rubbish bin. After giving me a panic attack, they climbed back inside it. Liam said they took their dead and dying with them. Incredibly, when he emptied the trash into the wheelie bin outside, there was not a single rat to be seen.'

The psychiatrist finished taking his notes and then looked her in the face again. 'You really do have the most incredible imagination Ms King. The faculty for creating mental images and non-rational associations can be useful in certain circumstances, such as for writers, artists and composers. It can also be harmful. You must learn to recognise the difference between what's real and what your mind's made up.'

So that was it. He was back to his usual humourless, tactless, cynical self. Good old Dr Wright. He did not believe a single word she told him. To make matters worse, the place still stank of perspiration.

'But it's all true,' she objected. 'Much of what I've told you was witnessed by other people as well. Take the seagulls on the beach for example, dozens of people saw them.'

He sported his usual smug expression. 'I think you're underestimating the number. Seagulls are witnessed by thousands of people in a seaside resort like Brighton. There's nothing strange about it.'

'There is when they start to attack you,' Faye tried to make him see. 'I'm not just talking about them stealing fish and chips. It was full-on warfare.'

Wright stood up. Towering over her made him even more intimidating. 'Let me remind you that you've come to see me to sort out your panic attacks. One of the things which brings on your phobia is being stared at. The first thing you can do is to give up your absurd desire to take your clothes off in front of other people. No wonder people stare at you. Public nudity is disgusting, as millions of conventional, decent people would agree.'

'Naturism is perfectly normal,' she argued back. 'We are all born naked and only dress because man-made laws say we must and to protect ourselves from the cold.'

This was all she could think of saying off the top of her head. She regretted that Liam was not there, as he had introduced her to naturism. He could so easily have explained the tremendous physical and mental benefits of the lifestyle.

The unfriendly doctor pointed to the door. 'I don't need a lecture thank you, about your silly ideas. Use some common sense and follow the advice I've given you. You can go now.'

Sniffing back tears, as she always did by the time her consultations with him had finished, she made her way out. Feet shuffling, she felt so down.

Only one thing had changed. Her dislike for Dr Wright was greater than ever.

Faye knew nothing about his background, but neither did his other clients. He made sure of that. His uncompromising bias against nudity was discreetly attributable to an emotional wound. It stretched back to his childhood.

As a youngster, he had developed Psoriasis, probably inherited from his father. A lifelong skin condition with no complete cure, it could sometimes flare up for months. The pink and red patches with white scales normally appeared on his elbows, knees, lower back and in the groin area. He was fortunate that his face, neck and hands were not affected. Providing he kept the rest of his body covered, his secret in adult life was hidden.

He had suffered terrible humiliation and bullying at school, however. Sports sessions and communal showers had been a nightmare. Other youngsters would point at his inflicted skin and pretend to vomit. The patches often being itchy and sore, he was cruelly nicknamed Scratchy.

This disease led to gymnophobia, the abnormal and persistent fear of nudity. His anxiety and distress at being seen without clothes ruled out intimacy and sexual relationships, forcing him to live a chaste life.

He began to worry about seeing others naked too, as it made him feel inferior. As a psychiatrist, he knew the phobia was irrational but his prejudice against nudists had multiplied over the years. It had got out of all proportion. His belief was that the naked human body was vulgar and should never be exposed to view.

Wright was a coward at heart, but outwardly he was callous, tactless and unethical.

Liam had waited outside the surgery again, phoning his friend, Jason. It gave him the chance to tell him about the disastrous naked bike ride.

When Faye arrived, Jason wanted to speak to her.

Liam handed over the phone.

'How was your session with Dr Wright?' he asked.

'No better than before,' she moaned. 'There's something terribly wrong with the man. He can't surely treat his other clients like he does me. The surgery would be inundated with complaints.

Jason was sorry to hear the appointment was unhelpful. 'I'm afraid I need to talk to you about something even more important. I must warn you about a certain type of psychic attack. Assaults do not just manifest on the material plain, but on other levels of consciousness too.'

She was following what he was saying as best she could. 'Such as?'

'In dreams for example,' he explained. 'It's quite possible for an attack to take the form of a vivid nightmare, whilst you're sleeping. You need to be on your guard. They won't necessarily be figments of your imagination.'

'You should try and persuade Wright of that,' she suggested. 'He thinks everything I tell him is just my imagination running riot.'

'We should never dismiss the image-making faculty. It serves many important functions. That's for discussion another time, however. Dreams, especially longer and more vivid ones, take place during altered states of consciousness, during the REM stage of sleep.'

'What's REM?' it was necessary for her to ask.

'It stands for Rapid Eye Movement, when the brain becomes very active. Have you ever heard of something called *Dream Walking*?'

'Is it anything to do with sleepwalking?' she wrongly

supposed.

'No. That's something different. Sleepwalking is getting out of bed and walking whilst still deeply asleep. Basically, dream walking on the other hand is when someone enters another person's dream space. It can be done voluntarily as shared dreaming, resulting in two people having precisely the same dream. The immoral side of dream walking is when one makes a conscious decision to enter their target's consciousness, whilst they're asleep. Their intention is to take complete control of the dream, including the setting and the dreamer's actions and responses.'

Faye was intrigued, having never heard of such a thing. 'Can anyone do this?'

'Not at all,' he made clear. 'One needs knowledge, willpower and a lot of practice. Dream walking should never be done without the other person's full consent. The person who we're sure is attacking you, however, won't give a damn about your permission. They have already built a strong connection with you, through previous attacks, which makes it easier for them. They don't even have to be asleep themselves, only in a deep meditative state. On the other hand, when you're in the dream state you are at your most open and vulnerable.'

Faye was naturally concerned to hear this. 'How do I prevent it happening?'

He disappointed her. 'You probably won't be able to. There are banishing and protection rituals, but they take proper training to be beneficial. You could, however, bring yourself out of a dream if it gets horrendously bad. Do you know anything about lucid dreaming?'

She shook her head, forgetting for a moment that she was talking down the phone.

Her lack of a reply still signalled a *no* to him. 'Lucid dreaming is when you realise you're dreaming, whilst in a dream. If this happens, you can hopefully then have some control over the dream. If you don't like it, you can change the direction it's going in, or even the whole scenario. You can alternatively wake yourself up, back into full consciousness.'

Faye was not at all sure of her capabilities when it came to this sort of thing. 'What if I'm unable to?'

'Your antagonist must be highly skilled,' he warned. 'They won't make it easy for you. Their intent will be to torment you and to let it play on your subconscious. Anxiety, fear and terror can be used as weapons against you. Never underestimate. Nightmares can be extremely dangerous. They can lead to mental and physical health problems, even to an increased risk of suicide. Remember what I've said, as all your weaknesses will be exposed. Most important of all, never dismiss what you experience as mere fantasy!'

'But the psychiatrist told me to do precisely the opposite,' she pointed out.

'Well, he's a fool,' Jason made clear. 'Ignore every suggestion he's made. If you don't, things could get extremely dangerous.'

12

'We must get a good night's sleep,' Liam insisted. 'We've got to be up early.'

Faye's bewildered expression suggested she had forgotten why.

He nudged her memory. 'Don't you remember? We're going to some gardens. We booked weeks ago, before all the trouble we've been having started.'

With everything that had happened, it had completely slipped her memory. 'Whatever for?'

'It's an organised trip. The gardens are attached to an old manor house. They're supposed to be fantastic. Best of all, for tomorrow only, they are going to be naturist friendly. We can leave all our clothes on the coach and explore them as nature intended. I managed to get hold of a couple of spare tickets from the naturist club, who've organised everything.'

'I hope Jason and Scarlet are coming with us,' she enthused. 'It sounds fun.'

He disappointed her. 'I'm afraid not. They're both busy. The coach is picking us up outside the Dome on Church Street at 9am. We'll need to take our towels and suntan lotion, but there's a small café in the gardens, where we can get lunch.'

'Where exactly are these gardens?' She was hoping they would not be too far away, as she disliked long coach journeys.

Surprisingly, he did not know. 'Your guess is as good as mine. The naturist club have kept it a surprise for their members and guests. They just said it was a naturist mystery day trip to beautiful manor house gardens.'

'Presumably, we'll get to see inside the manor house too,' she hoped.

He knew this was not possible. 'When booking, they made it clear that it was only the outside grounds we could roam around. The enormous manor house has been closed to visitors for years and is now completely derelict. No one's allowed inside for safety reasons. Perhaps the owner's opening the gardens to help raise money for its restoration.'

She thought it sounded rather creepy. 'What about the weather? Suppose it's raining all day?'

On this he could at least be more positive, having already checked the forecast. 'We're in luck there at least. Unbroken sunshine's predicted.'

That night, Faye must have been thinking about the next day's adventure, as she drifted off to sleep.

Later, during the REM part of her sleep cycle, as Jason had described it, she saw herself sitting on the coach, with Liam beside her.

Leaving behind the streets of Brighton, they travelled along busy roads and motorways for some time. Her head slumped onto his shoulder, the motion and whooshing of the wheels sending her into even deeper sleep.

After stopping and starting at traffic lights and junctions, the coach eventually slowed down.

Realising they were in the countryside she opened her eyes.

The road was much narrower, without markings. Green grass grew either side of it. Hedgerows and barbed wire fencing separated it from farmers' fields, most dotted with trees. Gaps in the foliage revealed crops or grazing cattle and sheep.

Occasional cars pulled over, allowing the coach to squeeze by. Ahead of them, a tractor crossed the road, throwing up billows of dust in its wake.

As they turned into a side road, the sound from the vehicle's wheels changed again, to that of crunching gravel. A hand painted sign, black on white, read *Gardens open for naturists only today*.

Pulling up in front of the café, everyone keenly stripped off their clothes. With footwear only, one by one they disembarked the coach.

It was not necessary to stay as a group and so Liam and Faye explored the gardens at their own pace. They really were beautiful. Their eyes were treated to a vast spectrum of colour, from an incredible variety of annual and perennial flowers.

As they ambled along the winding paths, their nostrils caught the scents of so many sweet-smelling perfumes. Their ears gave audience to the harmonised hum of bees, the delicate fluttering of wings and the joyous acoustics of birdsong.

They rested for a while, sitting on an old wooden bench by a largish fishpond. Intrigued by the orangey-yellow goldfish, with their long-flowing fins, they admired such graceful swimming.

As they walked on, they passed interesting weather-beaten sculptures, which looked as if they had been there for centuries. There were flowering shrubs, bushes and trees everywhere, all brimmed with the freshness and vitality of creation.

Unfolding their towels, they lay side by side in a meadow of freshly mown grass. The sun shone down on them, through the cloudless blue sky. It was glorious. If only earthly bliss like this was eternal.

Faye must have dozed for a while, for when she opened her eyes Liam was no longer there. Neither was his towel.

Wondering if he had gone to the café, to fetch them a snack, or to use the facilities, she went in search of him. She did not think to take her towel and had left everything else on the coach for safekeeping, even her mobile phone. Liam had been taking the photos, using his.

Being stark naked, all she had with her were her sandals. If only she had learned from the mistakes she had made in the disastrous bike ride.

Liam was nowhere to be found. Thinking he had maybe gone to look at the outside of the old, dilapidated manor house, she headed in that direction.

Frozen in time and unmaintained for decades, the boarded-up property was massive. The previous owners must have been extremely wealthy, before they finally ran out of money. Whoever they were, their former home was now decidedly menacing and uninviting.

Unlike the spectacular gardens, the once great house was surrounded by mostly dead trees and plants. This alone made it even more eery. It was as if nothing would grow near it. She started to circle the paint-peeling exterior walls, stepping over tiles which had fallen from the steeply pitched roof.

Every door and window was securely boarded. Several vivid black-on-yellow *Danger! Keep Out!* signs were displayed.

It was around the back and completely out of sight that she passed a small door. To her utter surprise it was ajar. There would have been just enough room for her to squeeze through, had she wanted. She had no intention of going inside. Even the idea scared her.

Instead, she shouted through the gap. 'Liam? Are you in there? If you are, you shouldn't be. You know we were told not to go inside the manor house.'

She waited for a response, but none came.

Faye tried again, much louder and a little nearer. 'Liam! If you're in there, come out now. I'm worried about you.'

Still nothing, so she popped her head through the opening.

It was too dark inside to see anything. 'Liam? Where are you?'

A single step forward took her partially inside the doorway. She was not going any further. 'Liam! Come out at once if you're in here.'

Without any warning at all, the door suddenly slammed shut behind her.

The impact, as it hit her back, threw her forward, onto her hands and knees.

She screamed at the top of her voice.

No one heard her.

With the door closed it was pitch black. She could not see a thing.

Pulling herself to her feet, she turned and fumbled at the door, trying to find a handle, or some other opening fixture.

Running the palms of her hands over the plain inner surface, she could not find anything.

Shoving the door with all her might had no effect at all. Neither did bashing it with her shoulder or kicking at it. The thing was rock solid. It refused to move.

Faye was mortified. She had always been fearful of the dark. It had terrified her since childhood, especially when she was alone. Dr Wright had told her it was called nyctophobia or something. It was just another of the many phobias which plagued her.

Why was she sweating? It was far too cold in such a deathtrap for perspiration.

Her heart was pounding too. Her mouth dry. What if she fainted, passed out, lost consciousness? Would she ever be found? What if she were to die in this stinking darkness?

Desperately, she banged the door again, thumping on it repeatedly with both fists. 'Help me someone! Open this fucking door! Let me out! I'm trapped in this hellhole! I need help!'

No one was in the vicinity to hear her.

At least not on the outside of the door!

Ensnared in a tomb-like silence, Faye was shaking like a leaf.

With difficulty, she took some deep breaths, to try and calm herself. She had to think straight. It was her only hope. If the door would not open, another way out had to be found. Now. Straight away. Before it was too late.

Arms stretched out in front; she took a tentative step forward.

Thank heavens she was at least wearing her sandals. Goodness knows what she was walking on. It could be anything. From the foul smell it might even be a layer of excrement. The thought almost made her vomit.

When the door had slammed, her hands had broken her fall.

She held the slimy palms to her nose. Hell did they stink, but she had nothing to wipe them on. Why had she not had the foresight to pick up her towel when she had gone looking for Liam?

Moving forward, she took one careful step at a time.

Her hand hit something, right in front of her.

It felt solid. A wall perhaps?

She examined it with both hands. Her path blocked, the only option would be to move sideways, either to her left or right.

For no reason, she chose the latter.

Finding a gap, she prayed it was an open door.

Tentatively, she shuffled through it.

A tiny crack of light showed in the distance.

Heading for it, she banged her knee on something hard. It hurt. She cursed but at least managed to keep her balance.

Cautiously manoeuvring herself around whatever it was, she carried on towards the light.

It seemed to be coming from a boarded-up window. There was a small gap between the frame and the square of wood nailed to it.

She leaned in to take a closer look.

Her body jerked back. She was covered in something.

The piercing scream which shot from her mouth must have echoed through the entire mansion. 'No, no, not that,' she whimpered, realising what it was.

Sticky, silky threads clung to her face. It was a spider's web!

Heart rate soaring again, she frantically attempted to pull the strands from her lips.

Stupid idea. The reeking slime from her fingertips was now all over her mouth. The pungent stench, just beneath her nostrils, made her vomit.

Bitter, gooey, putrid spew gushed from her mouth, splattering her naked skin.

Some of it running down her chin, she went to wipe it from her mouth.

Just in time, she remembered having already made the same mistake.

Instead, she grasped at her long-flowing hair, using it as a wipe.

As Dr Wright was aware, spiders were near the top of the list when it came to her greatest fears. It was a further phobia in her portfolio of embarrassment.

Perched in the corner of its web, the ghastly spider had been waiting patiently for her to enter its trap. The vibrations from her trembling body alerted it of her intrusion.

Now, its eight long hairy legs started their prowl towards her face. It was hunting her down. Slowly sneaking up on her, in expectancy of finding its next meal.

Faye knew all about spiders. She had done the research. They are carnivorous. After trapping flies and other insects, they cocoon them in even more webbing. Like a sedative applied with a syringe, their needle-sharp fangs inject their prey with venom. Before they can swallow their quarry, they jab them again, but with digestive fluids. Slowly then, they suck out and savour the liquefied remains.

Panic stricken, she squealed.

The intricate network of skin nerves sensed the hairy spider crawling leg by leg over her face.

Then, it stopped dead still.

She held her breath.

What kind of spider was it? It felt massive. What would it do to her? Suppose it had enough poison to kill her?

It moved again.

She screwed up her eyes in terror. Had it been lighter and her eyes open, she would have made out its own eyes. All six, or maybe eight of them, glimmering their eerie glow.

Backing away from the window, she side-stepped further to her right.

Another big mistake.

Unbeknown to her, she was now in the corner of the room. She had walked right into innumerable cobwebs.

Her entire juddering nude body was covered in them.

In vain, she tried to escape but was tangled from head to foot.

Spider after spider scrambled over her skin. She had once read that there are fifty-two thousand, three hundred and nine known species of spiders. It felt as if every one of them was on her now.

In sheer desperation, she frantically shook her limbs, trying to dislodge those crawling up from the ground.

Stamping with her sandals, she crushed as many as she could. The darkness hid the blue blood which spurted from them.

Though in total distress, she knew it would be fatal for her to panic. If she fainted and fell, the spiders would envelope her completely. Some felt only the size of a pinhead, but the larger ones that of a huge hairy coconut.

Completely tangled in so many webs, they clambered over her breasts, their bristly legs tickling her nipples.

Several scaled the inside of her legs, heading towards her groin. Her whole body quivered. What if one, or several, managed to squeeze inside her?

Head swimming with dizziness, she forced herself to move.

Longer strides took her to another wall.

She found what felt like a door. It was closed.

Urgently, her hands sought a way to open the barrier.

Finding a knob, she turned it.

The door swung ajar.

Sighing in never ending relief, more light hit her eyes.

Squinting, ahead of her she could make out a long corridor.

Only one thought ran through her mind.

Please, please, please, let it be a way out!

13

Faye stumbled along the corridor. As she did so, her fingers continuously scraped at her skin and frantically pulled at her hair.

She managed to dislodge some of the spiders, but others defiantly clung on.

The further she went, the more she began to shiver. It was not only from fear, for the temperature had plummeted.

An instantaneous but mysteriously noiseless wind turned the air as cold as a tombstone. The biting chill cut against her naked skin.

Hunching her neck, she tensed up, rubbing her shoulders. The hairs on her arms, legs and torso stood up straight, as goosebumps formed. Body jittering, teeth chattering, it was as if she had fallen into an icy crevasse. Her heart pumped faster, struggling to circulate the blood through her near frozen body.

Out of the until-then silence came the haunting and distressing sound of a woman sobbing. The lifeless emotion behind the weeping suggested not just sadness, but also sheer hopelessness.

Faye assumed she was not supposed to be listening.

This was not her locality. The crying was not meant for her ears. It was the private and solitary despair of some other poor soul.

Her heart leapt. Someone was whispering her name.

'Faye? Faye? Faye? Is that you Faye? I've been looking for you.'

'Liam!' she hollered back. 'You've come to save me. I'm here Liam, right here, in this freezing passageway.'

'Who is Liam?' came a stark reply.

She had been mistaken. The voice belonged to someone else.

'Stop walking at once!' It sounded furious. 'You stand right there and listen to me. You're nothing but a bitch!'

Something touched her shoulder. It felt like a hand and almost scared her to death.

She looked all around. There was no one to be seen.

This time her back was brushed, making her flinch.

Someone stroked her head; another grabbed her arm.

'Get off me,' she wailed. 'Leave me alone.'

The invisible and unknown touchers were undeterred. She was pushed, pulled, prodded, and mauled. Her bare breasts were groped, her backside fondled.

Filled with sudden alarm at this physical assault, she felt something lingering at the top of her leg. It was not one of the spiders.

Her protective reflex thrust her own hand over her sex, barring whatever it was from entry. Scared witless, her knees went weak.

It was sheer determination and her survival instinct which made her sprint on. 'Don't you dare assault me,' she demanded. 'You've no right.'

The response was immediate.

Boisterous wails of menacing laughter bombarded her ears. At the same instant, glaring lights began to flash on and off.

As she ran, her arm part-shielding her eyes, she glanced to either side.

Fleeting glimpses of her surroundings were revealed. Patches of black damp mildew covered the masonry. Mould-covered wallpaper peeled from the walls. The cause of the unpleasant musty smell of rotting plaster and wood was explained. Pile after pile of dead decomposing flies littered the dirty worn carpet.

Most alarming of all, were the dusty taxidermies. Stuffed wildlife animal heads were mounted high on the walls. If these cruel hunters' trophies could speak, she wondered, what sad tales they would tell.

Relief! Faye had at last reached the end of the long passageway. As she did so, a large door flew open right in front of her. Constant welcoming light and heat poured out through it.

'I'm saved!' she gasped aloud. 'I'm going to be alright!'

Darting through the opening, what she saw brought her to an abrupt standstill.

She was in a very large and busy kitchen, bustling with staff. They were so engrossed in their work that no one seemed to notice her. The obvious head chef was yelling commands at everyone, backed up by what must have been his sous chef. Whilst the prep cooks were busy getting the ingredients ready, several line cooks were preparing the dishes. Strong odours of garlic and curry powder, along with roasting and frying meat and vegetables filled the air.

A creeping sense of unease filled Faye's mind. She was trying to justify the existence of such an active kitchen in a derelict mansion house. She had thought the building was completely uninhabited, except for spiders and scary things more suited to a funfair's haunted house. The tiny cafe by the entrance to the gardens could surely not need such an enormous cooking facility.

Her suspicions aroused; her eyes bulged, and her jaw dropped, at the most spine-chilling and nauseous thing she had ever seen.

It was the integral ingredient of all the dishes which were being prepared. Near to where she was standing was the open door of a large walk-in refrigerated cold room. Hanging inside it, on hooks like string puppets, were carcasses. None of them were sides of beef, or some other dead animal. They were all clearly human corpses. Some were intact, but others were missing their head or limbs. Beneath them ran an overflowing trough, the receptacle to catch their dripping blood.

Aghast at such a sight, she turned away, her stomach heaving. She had to get away.

It was too late. She had been spotted and quickly surrounded. Several of the staff barred her escape.

A tall, mean-looking man stepped towards her. His white uniform was spattered with blood. In one hand he held a heavy broad-bladed cleaver.

He looked her naked body up and down. 'What have

we here?'

Stroking his chin whilst trying to decide, he called for the head chef.

The pot-bellied executive, pinnacle of the kitchen's hierarchy, wandered over slowly. His nose held high in a snobby manner; a burning cigarette hung from the corner of his mouth.

Taking a drag, he removed it between his middle and forefinger, blowing a cloud of smoke into Faye's face.

She stepped back to avoid it.

'What's wrong dear? Don't you approve of smoking?' There was sarcasm in his voice.

She did not reply. His unhealthy addiction was the last of her concerns. This was clearly his empire. He was the one who made the rules.

Placing the cancer stick back in his mouth, he gave her his own inspection. 'You're most welcome, young lady, especially completely naked like this.'

He realised how dirty her skin and hair were. 'You're going to need a good wash. Your prettiness and perfect body don't quite camouflage the filth you're covered in. There are also spiders crawling on you. We must maintain good hygiene.'

He poked at her with his finger. 'You've got a nice lean body. Hardly any fat on you at all. Whether the diners choose leg or breast, you're going to go down very well.'

Terror stricken, she tried to push past the cooks, but they held her tight. 'Let me go! There's been a big mistake. I'm not supposed to be here.'

'You're certainly not part of our usual delivery,' the

chef humoured, 'but we never turn down additional supplies of meat. It's surprising how many visitors to the gardens ignore the *Danger, Keep Out* signs. We'll get the Slaughterer to hose you down.'

He pointed to the person opposite.

Faye squealed, recognising him immediately. It was the bald giant who had attacked her in the sauna's hot tub and had also knocked her to the ground in the naked bike ride!

He was dressed exactly as before, in the same long-sleeved shirt and dark trousers. Now though, he had an apron tied in front of his belly. No doubt originally white, spilt blood had turned it crimson. Just like before, his bulging eyes stared threateningly into hers.

Just the sight of him filled her with terror.

The head chef noticed her reaction. 'You're right to be scared. He never says a word, but his actions speak for themselves. We call him the Slaughterer, as that's what he does. With a name like that for a slayer, who needs a job description.'

His words caused chilling laughter from his colleagues.

'He's an evil bastard,' the chef continued. 'The more pain he can inflict during a killing, the more he likes it!'

She struggled again to break from those holding her, but they were not letting her go.

'Take her to the shower,' he instructed the Slaughterer, 'and the rest of you get back to work. We've got food to prepare. There are hungry customers waiting to be fed.'

As she was dragged away to the far corner of the kitchen, she breathed in the sickly smell of death, the stench of cooking human flesh.

She passed the most shocking sights imaginable. Laid out bodies were being butchered. They were skinned and disembowelled. Innards and entrails were carefully put to one side for offal dishes. Saws cut through carcasses, halving and quartering them. Sharp knives sliced through flesh.

Hosed down and soaking wet, Faye saw the Slaughterer pick up a large carving knife. She knew she had no chance of overpowering him. Her height, build and muscles were diminutive compared to his. So many other depraved kitchen staff would come to his aid anyway. She was outnumbered and on her own. No one was coming to her rescue.

The Slaughterer raised his knife, ready to plunge it into her.

She did not want to die, especially at the hands of such a sadist fiend. Her mind switched to fight or flight mode. Her body flooded with adrenaline and blood rushed through her muscles.

It was her turn now to look him straight in the eyes. In doing so, she deliberately avoided looking down. It would have given him a hint of her defence. She would have gone for his groin, but his height made it difficult.

Instead, with all her might, she kicked at the inside of his leg, just above the knee.

Although her foot hit the common peroneal nerve, no pain registered on his face. It did make him stagger though.

Losing his grip on the weapon, it fell to the floor.

Whilst he bent down to retrieve it, she dashed to a towering pile of poorly stacked kitchen supplies.

Summoning all her strength, she kicked repeatedly at one of the largest lower containers.

Thankfully, it finally gave way and rolled out.

Weight distribution unbalanced, she saw the stack waver and lean precariously. Gravity did the rest.

As she dashed for the door, she heard the entire high-reaching stock crash to the ground.

Some hit the Slaughterer, knocking him flat. Plastic vessels of olive oil burst open. Bottles of cognac and other flammable liquids smashed into pieces. The contents splattered onto the open flames from the stovetops and grills.

In such intense heat, virgin olive oil reached its flash point rapidly, bursting into flame.

Spilled strong spirits ignited.

Overheated gas cylinders exploded. Everything flammable was set on fire.

The blaze spread almost instantly to the human fat covered work surfaces, to dirty equipment, oven hoods and grease traps. The sound of the inferno roared, as it raged through the kitchen.

Intuitively, but foolishly, the head chef grabbed the hosepipe. He thought he could extinguish the fire with water. Instead, the spray only intensified the flames, steam spreading the burning grease particles even further.

Engulfed in a lethal, unstoppable, scorching firestorm, cooks and other kitchen staff burnt like paraffin-drenched human torches. They screamed in agony, but no sound came from their throats. The deadly thick black smoke had paralysed their throats.

Faye stood for a moment at the door she had first entered through. Anxiously, she surveyed the result of her bid for freedom.

Satisfied that everything was being destroyed, she sprinted into and along the passageway, away from the kitchen.

Glancing back, she could see smoke pouring into the rest of the building.

As she raced past the stuffed animal heads on the wall, she heard them shout out to her. 'Run Faye.' 'Run!' 'You must escape!' 'Don't die like we did!' 'We were slaughtered, but you must live!' 'Run Faye!' 'Run!'

Their frantic vocalisations made no sense to her. Dead animals only talk, especially in the human tongue in movies and in dreams. This was no movie.

The realisation hit home. She must be having a dream.

She recalled Jason telling her how dangerous nightmares could be. He had explained about dream walking. How someone evil could get into your dream without your permission and control it. He had mentioned something called lucid dreams. He had most importantly told her how to escape from a dream.

With the whole manor house now ablaze, she stopped running.

Her mind had gone blank. She had to think clearly. What was it that he had said?

She had to remember!

14

'Did you sleep all right?' Liam asked Faye the next morning.

'To start with perhaps,' she told him. 'But I had an extremely terrifying nightmare.'

He was curious, especially knowing that Jason had warned her about certain types of dreams. 'Can you still remember it?'

'It's one I'll never forget.' From the anxious look she gave him, it seemed even talking about it was distressing. 'We're supposed to go on that day trip to the manor house gardens today,' she knew. 'Do you mind if we stay here instead?'

'We can't go anyway,' he explained.

He handed her his mobile phone. 'You'd better read the message I got earlier. It's from the organiser, the guy from the naturist club.'

Pressing the text icon, she read it. Her face drained of colour.

She read the message again, this time aloud. '*Sorry. Today's trip cancelled. Gardens sealed off by police, investigating major incident last night. The old manor house was burnt to the ground.*' Her voice was shaky.

Liam was surprised by her reaction. 'It's not what we were expecting, but if you didn't want to go, it's a fortunate coincidence.'

Due to utter shock, she was unable for a moment to summon words. Instead, she read the message once more, but to herself.

She took his hand. 'I'm frightened. What if I tell you that I already knew about the manor house fire?'

This confused him. 'You've only just woken up, so how could you have heard?'

'I was there. In my dream.' Her eyes were welling up. 'I started the fire. It was my fault. I was trying to escape.'

What she was saying made no sense at all, but he put his arm around her protectively, as he always did when she was upset. 'You'd better tell me all about it, even if it was a dream.'

Her recollection of the nightmare was incredibly detailed. She recounted travelling to the gardens with him on the coach, her search for him and how she had become trapped inside the manor house. She shuddered again at her encounter with the spiders, at the weird and scary things in the passageway, her utter revulsion at what was in the kitchen and the identity of the Slaughterer. Describing how she managed to escape, as the fire enveloped the premises, she finished with the talking animal heads.

'It was them which made you realise you were dreaming?' he presumed.

'Yes, but then I had to try and remember Jason's instructions for getting out of a nightmare,' she recollected. 'Just in time I managed to wake myself up.'

Liam stated the obvious. 'It's just as well you did. But surely, if something happens in a dream, it doesn't mean it happens in waking life too. I think I'd better give Jason a call. Hopefully, he can pop round and give us his take on what's happened. You'll need to tell him everything.'

'You said yesterday that he and Scarlet were busy today,' she seemed to remember. 'It was the reason they couldn't have come on the trip with us.'

He knew Jason's meeting was not until the afternoon. 'I'll ask if he can possibly spare us a few minutes this morning.'

Jason was most concerned about Faye when Liam spoke to him. So much so that he was there in less than half an hour.

Giving her a friendly kiss on the cheek, he asked her if she was all right.

'I'm still feeling rather shaken,' she admitted. 'I'll make you a coffee and then describe what's happened.'

'How's Scarlet?' Liam asked

'Fine,' Jason let him know. 'She's got her jewellery stall in the Open Market today. The one near the London Road shops.'

Liam knew the place. 'Let's hope she has plenty of customers.'

'She usually does quite well there,' his friend confirmed. 'The daily rent in the central Plazza's very reasonable. They even provide the stall frames and tabletops. There used to be an excellent bookshop in one corner, but sadly the owner died. It's a real shame. He was a nice guy and stocked so many interesting and collectable second-hand books.'

'Has Liam told you about the text he received this morning?' Faye asked, when she came back with their coffees.

'Briefly,' Jason affirmed, 'when he phoned me. It must have come as a great shock. You'd better recount your dream and then we can try and analyse it.'

The whole nightmare remained incredibly clear in her mind. She had still not forgotten a thing, telling him about the initial journey and right through to the talking animal heads. 'So, what do you make of it all?'

Jason sipped his drink. 'Before we go any further, let's talk about the type of experience I think you had. Dreams which give us a glimpse into the future are known as precognitive dreams. They allow us to see events which have not yet occurred. Science can't prove or disprove them, but there's plenty of evidence they occur. So many people for example have predicted natural disasters before they happened. According to studies, thirty-eight per cent of people have at least one premonition dream in their lives. The psychologist Carl Jung, who did a lot of work on dream interpretation, is believed to have had several himself.'

'If there are so many,' she reasoned, 'why are premonitions not more widely accepted.'

'They are seen by some to violate causality, the theory which describes the relationship between cause and effect. Although it's not scientific law, it claims there must be a cause for every effect. The problem with predictive dreams is that the opposite seems to occur. The effect happens before the cause.'

She did not quite follow. 'But I dreamed not just of the fire, but of its cause too and then it turned out to have happened in real life.'

'Those who don't believe in predictive dreams would argue that the cause you dreamed of was not the real one. Hopefully, the investigators will eventually discover how the manor house burnt down. It will be most interesting if the police and fire service come up with evidence that it started in a working kitchen.'

'I could save them a great deal of time,' she insisted, 'by admitting I was there. It was me who accidentally started the fire, when I was trying to escape from the kitchen.'

'But it's highly unlikely they'd accept what you say as fact,' he knew. 'Under British law, you're not going to be charged with arson, over something you saw happen in a dream.'

Liam cut in. 'Are you saying the fire in her dream had nothing to do with the actual fire.'

'No. Not at all,' he was careful to distinguish. 'I'm simply pointing out what the non-believers of precognitive dreams would assume. Time must also be taken into consideration. Did the fire start in the night at about the same time as in your dream? Time as we know it always travels forward. There are some physicists however, who believe it flows backward as well as forwards. If so, this would help support your premonition. You experienced the fire through intuition. It's clearly had a great emotional impact on you, being so vividly clear and detailed. From your description it impacted on all your senses, from sight and sound to smell and touch.'

'It's hardly surprising,' she agreed. 'I'm never going to forget any of it and especially what was happening in the kitchen.'

'Dreams embody symbolism. As I've mentioned before, it's the oldest language in the world,' he expounded. 'Fire in dreams is a very powerful symbol. It can represent passion, anger, destruction, or transformation. The uncontrollable fire no doubt signified your unrestrained emotions and phobias getting out of hand. As it caused you fear and anxiety, it was your subconscious telling you to be cautious. The warning of destruction represented loss, or endings in your life. As I made the point of telling you recently, ignoring dreams can make you vulnerable to all kinds of risks and dangers which might lay ahead.'

Knowing that Jason was a professional dream interpreter, as well as a tarot card reader, gave credence to everything he was telling her.

'Why would there be cannibalism in my dream?' she asked. 'As far as I know, it's not one of my phobias.'

'The fear of cannibalism is known as ososphobia,' he enlightened her. 'It's derived from the Greek word for human-eater. Cannibalism is one of civilisation's greatest taboos. The thought of people eating human flesh disgusts us. We can only really tolerate the subject in fictional horror stories or films. In those settings we know the characters aren't ordinary, real or sane human beings. Even if they're portrayed as such, we know we're safe and protected from them.'

'The same would go for violence as well,' Liam suspected, 'which goes hand in hand with cannibalism.'

'There are all sorts of situations where violence is seen,' Jason acknowledged. 'There's certainly plenty of it on television and in films. Strangely, violence seems to be accepted as good entertainment, whilst any portrayal of nudity or sex can be scorned at. Ironically, it seems many people would prefer watching humans kill each other, rather than seeing them in their natural state, or making love.'

He was keen to get back to the subject of Faye's dream. 'The violence in your dream suggested changes in your life. It made you defensive in the dream and will hopefully help make you defensive in waking life. It's also symbolic of the specific struggles and adversities you have. We all have weaknesses, some perhaps wrongly perceived, as well as challenges to be resolved.'

'I've got plenty of them,' she fully accepted. 'I must surely suffer more phobias than the average person. Dr Wright thinks so anyway. He called it polyphobia. The spiders last night really freaked me out.'

Jason understood. 'The obvious symbolism of spiders in dreams relates to you being overwhelmed and anxious. Their webs signify being trapped in nasty situations. They also represent deceit and the web of lies which surround you. There is however a positive side to encounters with spiders, even in dreams. As in the wide-awake world, the females are usually larger, more powerful and live longer than the males. They know how to defend themselves from danger, as you did in the kitchen within your dream. Spiders also signify the need for you to sort out your fears. It's obvious to me that your phobias are being used against you, to cause you harm.'

'The manor house was more like the haunted houses in horror films and novels,' she thought. 'The temperature plunged to freezing. Then came flashing lights, weird noises, a voice calling my name, invisible hands touching me up and stuffed animals talking.'

'All these experiences were conveying something to you,' he stressed. 'The talking wild animal heads were really your own unconscious mind, guiding you and encouraging you to escape. It was not only from the burning building, but also from all the negativity, fears and challenges you face. Symbolising wisdom, intuition and insight, they were urging you to have a deeper connection with your own instinct and to listen to your inner voice. It was only when you did this that you finally realised you were in a dream.'

'Without the stuffed animals I would have perished in the fire,' she feared.

Jason was not so sure, but he did need to remind her again of the importance of nightmares and dreams. 'Don't forget my warning about dream walking, where an enemy can get into and control your dreams. The Slaughterer, whom you recognised as being the same fiend from the health spa and bike ride, was proof enough. Fortunately, your nightmare was a lucid dream. It was the kind where once you realised you were dreaming, you could wake yourself up.'

Faye breathed a sigh of relief. 'Which I finally remembered to do.'

Jason looked at his watch and got to his feet. 'I must be going. I've got a few more things to do before my meeting. First though, more warnings. Dreaming about cannibalism also signifies someone's hatred for you. You need to be extremely cautious. I told you recently that we were spying on a crazy Christian cult called the Guardians of Modesty. Although they're fanatically against any type of public nudity, they especially loathe female naturists. I've no doubt it's their leader who's behind all the attacks on you, but we're still trying to uncover the supernatural powers he must possess. You've got to be vigilant. You and Liam are still in great danger. Goodness knows what that madman, known as the Reverend, will try and do next!'

15

'What are we going to do for the rest of the day,' Faye asked Liam, 'now the coach trip's off?'

He was extremely surprised she wanted to go anywhere, considering what she had been through.

'With such lovely weather, there's always the beach,' he suggested.

From the frown on her face, she was not convinced. 'I still haven't forgotten what happened the last time we went to Brighton's naturist beach. There was the scam photographer, the maggot sandwiches and the killer seagulls. Then, we got home to find someone had entered the flat.'

None of this had escaped his mind either, but he was keen to try another beach. 'Fortunately, the flat's much more secure now, with the metal panel fitted on the frame. It would be very difficult for anyone to get in. As for the beach, I was thinking of the one in Portslade, just along the coast by Shoreham Port.'

He had mentioned this alternative location before but had never taken her there. 'It's a lot quieter than the other one,' he stressed, 'which means fewer seagulls for a start. We can have an early lunch here before we go.'

Whilst not dismissing the idea, she needed to know more. 'How easy is it to get to?'

'Quite simple,' he described. 'We can take the westbound 700 coastline bus and get off by Hove Lagoon. From there, a road leads down to it. Like Brighton, the beach is all shingle and pebbles, but a high sea wall separates it from Shoreham Harbour. This means there are no gawping passersby. As it's owned by Shoreham Port Authority, it's not officially classified as a public naturist beach, but it's been used by nudists for years.'

Thinking it would detract from her memories of the nightmare she agreed to give it a go.

As soon as they had eaten, they headed to Churchill Square and got the bus.

Twenty minutes later, they were standing by Hove Lagoon, watching the windsurfers and other water sport activities. An easy walk along Basin Road South took them to the wooden fenced beginning of the naturist beach.

Although it was a lovely, blue-skied afternoon, there were only a scattering of people on the beach. It was quiet, just as Liam had described.

The tide being in, after trudging along the pebbles they settled near to the high concrete wall. The westerly wind was very light, but Liam used a large stone to hammer in the poles of their blue and white windbreak. Having carried it from home, he was determined to make use of it, whether it was necessary or not.

Beach mats and towels laid, they both stripped off. Their bodies released from unnecessary clothing, they sensed as always, the delightful feeling of freedom. They felt the embracing warmth of the healing sun and the sensual caress of the gentle breeze. It was entirely what nature had intended to invigorate their naked skin.

Sensibly, they applied a liberal coating of sun lotion. In some ways, the greasy formula slightly spoilt the liberation. Nevertheless, its use was essential, especially with global warming.

Lying on their towels, propped up on their elbows, they surveyed the sea.

In the distance were the Rampion wind farm turbines. Some of the rotor blades were silently turning, generating renewable energy.

A cargo ship, probably carrying timber, headed for the entrance to the harbour. Meanwhile, other vessels waited patiently, queuing for their turn to load or unload freight.

Their eyes followed a boat on the horizon, which was moving ever-so-slowly in the opposite direction. Contemplating where it might be bound, they imagined it was to some far-flung exotic land, full of swaying palm trees and white sandy beaches. Much more likely, it was probably to somewhere far less exciting.

Their tranquillity was disturbed for just a few moments by the pulsating, chopping sound of a police helicopter as it flew overhead.

Faye remembered Liam saying it was an unofficial naturist beach. 'Are they spying on us?'

He very much doubted it. 'They'd be hovering if they were, but it's flown straight over. Don't forget that naturism is perfectly legal in the UK. Anyway, I'm sure the police have got far better things to do with their time than watch us sunbathing.'

'One would have hoped so,' she agreed.

He pointed out the Shoreham Power Station, just a short distance along the road to the west. Its tall chimney, a local landmark, dominated the skyline. 'It runs on natural gas,' he was able to inform her. 'Apparently, hot wastewater from it is released into the sea. Some say it makes it warmer to swim in, but I doubt it makes much difference.'

Faye got to her feet. 'I'll let you know. I'm going for a paddle.'

She had forgotten how lumpy the pebbles were and was soon back for her sandals. 'I'll keep them on in the water. They're only an old pair and very light.'

He watched, as she made her way to the water's edge.

'It's not bad at all,' she shouted back, as the tiny ripples covered her feet and ankles. 'I think it's even all right for a swim. Is it safe?'

Although there was no one else in the water, he had seen quite a few taking a dip when he had last been there. 'It should be, but don't go out too far.'

'I'll just skinny-dip to the wind farm turbines and back,' she kidded.

Wading up to her waist, she lowered her torso into the water, shivering. 'It's not like being in a warm bath exactly, but still rather refreshing.'

Taking the plunge, she dived forward into her usual front crawl.

Liam watched, as she propelled herself slowly through

the water. He so hoped their afternoon on the beach was doing her good. After all the stressful anxiety she had been subjected to, she so deserved some happiness and relaxation.

Whilst she was soon a little further out to sea than he had hoped, she was at least keeping to an area where he could still see her.

Faye was enjoying her swim. From the moment she lowered her body into the salt water, all her troubles faded. The awful memories of the night before dissolved into the vastness of the English Channel. For the first time in weeks, she was filled with exuberance. Had she been a marathon swimmer, her gusto alone could have easily taken her to France and back.

Suddenly, her exhilaration was cut short. Something had grabbed an ankle.

Bringing her to an abrupt and unpredictable stop, it was trying to pull her down.

She kicked out with both legs, desperately attempting to dislodge whatever was holding on to her.

Despite her efforts, it was unyielding.

Clasping her even tighter, it pulled harder and harder.

Her head about to be drawn beneath the surface, she just managed to gulp a mouthful of air.

Both of her arms desperately continued their swimming strokes. They were taking her nowhere. She was held fast.

Her heart began to race. She felt her chest tighten, realising the peril she was in. She needed to breathe. If she could not break free, she would drown.

This fight for survival activated her fight or flight response. It was the same physiological reaction she had experienced far too often recently.

Adrenaline triggered; the energy boost gave her hope. She fought with all her might. But not for long. Her body soon tired again, movements becoming quick and jerky. She was losing the battle to prevail. Her lungs ached so much for oxygen.

With the last of her strength and in one final effort, she pummelled her free leg against the one being held.

Mercifully, she was set free. She could move again, unrestrictedly.

Instinct alone immediately propelled her upward.

Thrusting her face above the surface of the water, she inhaled a mouthful of life-saving air.

Treading water, her legs moved in a peddling motion, her arms back and forward.

Impetuously, she looked all around.

There was no sign of whoever or whatever had attacked her. She could see Liam in the distance, relaxing on the beach. She so wanted to call out to him for help, but her lungs had other ideas. Their sole intention was to conserve vital oxygen, in case she was suddenly pulled under again.

She dared not signal to him either, knowing that raising her arms would cause her to sink.

Unwavering willpower urged her to swim to safety.

Synchronically, a strange voice was whispering for her not to do so.

Strange dark thoughts, that were not her own, swirled through her mind. It was as if an infiltrator had gate-crashed her brain and was dictating orders to her.

The demand was that she must stay there in deep water. On no account was she to leave. If she drowned everything would be wonderful, putting an end to all her problems. No more nightmares. No more attacks. No more worries. No more suffering from phobias. She was to set an example by ending her life. Her valiant self-sacrifice would be applauded. Naturists throughout the world would be inspired to follow her ultimate achievement. This was her true destiny, the real purpose of her life.

At that moment, Liam happened to open his eyes. His hand shielding them from the sun, they searched for sight of her.

The moment he spotted her upright in the water, her head bobbing up and down, he knew something was wrong.

He ran to the water's edge. 'Start swimming Faye!' he yelled.

Wading deeper, he shouted over and over. 'Swim Faye! Swim! You've got to swim!'

Hearing his cries brought her to her senses. She snapped out of the enchantment controlling her and started to think for herself.

Her limbs were tired, but they automatically slipped into swimming mode, carrying her towards the shore.

Soon, she was safely in his arms.

Tears streaming from her eyes, he helped her out of

the water and sat her safely on the pebbles.

'Whatever happened out there?' he asked anxiously. 'Are you alright?'

She wiped her eyes with the back of her hand. 'Something pulled me under. It gripped my ankle, but I managed to break free.'

He was staggered. 'Why didn't you at that point start swimming for the shore?'

'Something told me not to,' she said chillingly. 'It was as if I was in a hypnotic trance. A calming voice was convincing me I was supposed to drown. It said I would be setting a good example, one that other naturists would follow. It was only hearing you calling out to me which broke the spell and set me free.'

Confounded at hearing this, he knew it must be connected to all the other attacks she had suffered. 'Thank goodness I spotted you when I did and that you heard me. Did you swallow much water?'

Her reply came as a relief. 'Hardly any. It went up my nose of course, but it could have been a lot worse.'

'You must have been so frightened,' he rightly assumed.

She held out her hands. 'Look, I'm still shaking. I thought I was going to die.'

He held her close. 'Take a few deep breaths. You're safe now. You're back with me.'

'If I'd have drowned out there,' she whimpered, 'we'd have never seen each other again.'

He kissed her gently. 'But you didn't. You overcame whoever was trying to harm you. Nothing can separate us.'

'It was as if I was in the middle of another nightmare,' she tried to explain, 'but this time I was wide awake.'

Thoughts of the night before returning, she massaged her temples, trying to stop such a line of thought. 'I don't want to spoil your afternoon, but if you don't mind, I'd like to go home.'

Unfortunately, doing so was going to be more difficult than either of them thought.

16

Liam helped Faye to stand up. It was only then they noticed the sandal was missing from her right foot.

'You can hobble up to our things without it,' he reckoned, 'but you'll never manage to walk over the pebbles, especially to the end of the beach. It's too far for me to carry you.'

'I need to find it then,' she realised. 'There's no way I'm going back in the water though.'

He entirely agreed. 'Of course you're not. I'll look for it. Hopefully, it's been washed up into the shallows.'

While Faye headed to their things and dried herself off with her towel, Liam started his search. With no sign of her shoe by the water's edge, he walked deeper into the water.

He came to an area where the sea had turned much darker and murkier.

As he strode into it, an ever-so-strong, foul-smelling stench hit his nostrils. As his fingers held his nose, breathing through his mouth, something unexpected caught this eye. Floating on the surface were hundreds of human faeces. Turds of every size were swimming in the water.

The sight of so much bodily waste made him gag. Floating alongside all the stinking stools and ammonia-wafting urine, were several used sanitary towels, soiled babies' nappies and disintegrating dirty toilet wipes.

Nausea rising in his throat, he hastily made for the shore, wondering where so much excrement had come from.

Aware that his legs and feet were covered in the stinking sewage, he walked further along to where the water was clear. There he rinsed them.

It was there too that he found Faye's lost sandal. It had something attached to it. He feared the worst, but thankfully it was only a piece of seaweed.

Returning to Faye and handing her the shoe, he pointed down the beach to where he had found it and further along to where the sewage was. 'It was just as well you didn't swallow much seawater.'

'Please, don't even put the thought in my mind,' she begged. 'I'll have to wear the shoe home, but I'll give it a really good clean when we get there.'

'Our bodies are going to need an even better wash,' he added. 'I don't know where all that blackwater sewage came from. The water quality assessments are supposed to be excellent for this part of the coastline. There's an outlet pipe further along, but it's unlikely to have come from there. It's almost as if someone scooped up all the body waste from the sewage works and deliberately dumped it in the sea for me to wade in.'

As they were almost dressed, ready to leave for home,

Faye unexpectedly noticed what looked like a dog. It was charging along the beach towards them.

Liam felt his leg muscles tightening. Seeing the dog darting their way, instinct told him to flee.

Wisely, common sense said otherwise, as the animal's own inclination would be to chase him. With no place to hide, he knew he must stand still, sideways on and avoid any threatening moves.

He had learned this from counselling. Although he had never confessed it to Faye, fearing she might think less of him, he himself suffered from a phobia. Known as cynophobia, it was an extreme fear of dogs. It had started in childhood, after he was once caught in the middle of two fighting canines. For some years, even seeing a dog caused anxiety and even panic. He had learned to better control this reaction over the years but still felt trepidation if approached by a large one.

As the dog got closer, they could see it was a German Shepherd. The animal's intimidating size suggested it was a male. With black saddled fur over a tan body, the thickness and length on the neck area was almost suggestive of a lion's mane. It must have been in the sea, for it was drenched.

Coming to an abrupt stop a short distance from them, it did a mammal shake, dislodging the water droplets.

By now, Liam's veins were beating a visible pulse beneath the skin.

Faye, on the other hand seemed to be coping with the situation well. She was remarkably calm, considering the danger which faced them.

The dog's head was strong and chiselled, broad with a slightly domed forehead. Its two almond-shaped dark brown eyes stared fixedly at him. The two alert pointy ears were directed forward. They were signs of danger. Beneath its black nose, with lifted lip, an aggressive snarl revealed its lethal scissor-biting teeth.

Liam positioned himself in front of Faye.

Inside he was terrified. Cold shivers ran through his shoulders, but he was determined to hide his emotions. He had learnt that dogs can smell fear through the chemical signals produced by the body. Betraying body language can do the same. Such animals are highly intelligent, which makes them even more unpredictable.

It barked, making them both jolt.

Seeing their reaction. It thundered several repeated deep resonant barks, as a sign of dominance.

Liam's face turning ashen, he could feel his tendons standing out in his neck.

Faye was asking what they should do to escape, but at that moment he was unable to speak.

The carnivorous mammal approached them slowly.

Walking upright and stiffly, hair bristling, its head was slightly raised.

With tail held tight and rigid, it stopped and stared at them again, a long pink tongue licking the sides of its mouth.

Liam, now sweating, knew how dangerous dog bites could be. Tetanus injections or antibiotics were often necessary. Desperately, he tried to think of how they could defend themselves. If it came to the worst, they had the wooden poles from the windbreak. There was also the pointed metal shaft of their beach umbrella. Even picking these up though, could antagonise the dog and make it even angrier.

'Why is it trying to scare us?' Faye whispered to him. 'What have we done to attract its rage?'

Liam did not answer. He could smell its strong canine musky odour. His mind was busy picturing images of them being torn to pieces by its powerful jaws.

He recalled being told to keep calm, keep his own lips closed to submissively hide his teeth and ignore the dog by turning away. No fast movements.

Intent on protecting Faye, he wished he could create a barrier between them and the dog. The windbreak was still up, but being side on, the animal could simply walk around it.

The German Shepherd was watching them intently, one of its forelegs doubled up, ready for its next decisive step.

It was snarling, spittle dripping from its mouth.

Even from the short distance between them, they could smell its stinking bad breath, suggesting it suffered from serious dental disease.

Faye thought of something herself. 'No!' she said firmly, hoping it might be a familiar word to the dog. She had the sense not to yell the word too loudly, in case it frightened the animal.

Either it did not hear her or had not been trained to react to the command.

Liam bent down in slow motion and picked up a small

piece of driftwood. His hand gripped it so hard that his knuckles turned white.

With care, so as not to suggest he was going to attack the dog, he carefully threw it to one side. He was hoping the canine would think he was playing a game and go and retrieve it.

The dog's eyes followed the wood as it flew but then went straight back to Liam.

It was preparing to pounce.

Growling savagely, it made small lunging motions.

The attack was coming. It was about to leap onto them. To scratch and tear. To bite at their faces. To maul them to death.

At any moment.

Now!

Precisely then, a whistle sounded. It came from along the beach, to the west.

The German Shepherd turned its head in that direction. Then it resumed its attack position.

The high pitch whistle was heard again.

This time, with some obvious reluctance, the dog gave them one more forbidding look and dashed off in that direction.

Liam and Faye both sighed aloud in relief.

They peered into the distance, to where the dog was running. There, on the raised concrete walkway, next to the wooden fencing, was standing a man. He was wearing a full-length black coat and was making a *come* gesture to the dog.

'What was all that about?' Faye asked. 'Is someone

trying to scare us off going to naturist beaches?'

Liam was busy packing their things. He wanted to get off the beach straight away, just in case the dog decided to return. 'It certainly looks like it. What with everything that happened on Brighton's naturist beach and now this one.'

'If they wished us harm,' she was trying to work out, 'why did they call the dog off at the very last moment?'

'Perhaps they're saving us for something even worse,' he feared.

Neither of them had ever met or seen the man whom Jason had said was responsible for all the previous attacks. Perhaps they had spied him now, albeit in the distance. It was too far for them to be able to recognise him, should their paths cross in the future. Despite this, Liam was certain of one thing.

It had definitely been the Reverend!

17

'Hallelujah! Praise the Lord!'

The congregation raised their hands in the air, displaying their usual adoration.

None were aware that the Reverend, their beloved leader, was unhappy with them.

It was in fact much worse. He was furious.

As he stepped onto the rostrum, some were perplexed at his expression. His face had almost turned purple with rage.

'Hallelujah! Praise the Lord!' Their voices rang out again.

At that precise moment the Reverend did not give a damn about their Psalm inspired hurrahs. The cult he was leading had let him down badly. Their behaviour had been unforgiveable. They were supposed to be the Guardians of Modesty. Instead, they had acted more like the miser Ebenezer Scrooge, from the Dickens novel, A Christmas Carol.

'Brethren,' he addressed them coldly. 'The Lord has insisted that I refer you to the Good Book.

Opening his well-worn copy of the Bible, he started his rebuke with a quote. 'In Malachi 3:8, the last book of the Old Testament, it says: *Will a man rob God? Yet ye have robbed me. But ye say, wherein have we robbed thee? In tithes and offerings.* It is with much regret that we must address your tithes.'

From their uncomfortable looks, this was obviously a subject some of them would rather he did not discuss.

'Your tithes are, as you very well know, supposed to be one tenth of your income,' he reminded them. 'There are some amongst you however, who are cheating. You are falsifying information to the Church of your true earnings. This is not just a financial issue, like filling in an income tax return, but of great spiritual significance. By lying to God, you are demonstrating a lack of trust and veneration for him. It suggests your hearts are turned away from him, that personal fortune is of more importance to you.'

He paused, studying them one at a time. They were supposed to be his loyal followers. There was no need to ask which ones were guilty. It was perfectly obvious by their body language.

Some bowed their heads, not in prayer but in shame. Their deliberate downward gaze was to avoid his. Others shuffled their feet, feeling degraded. Mortified about having been found out, most wished they could hide or flee. Knowing that doing so would bring immediate attention to them, in a childlike manner they instead closed their eyes, pretending not to be there.

The Reverend was a cunning and calculating preacher. He made sure they thought it was their Saviour, rather than him, who was chastising them. 'Know this, from Proverbs: *Honour the Lord with your wealth, with the first fruit of your crops; then your barns will be filled to overflowing and your vats will brim over with new wine. My son, do not despise the Lord's discipline and do not resent his rebuke, because the Lord disciplines those he loves as a father the son he delights in.'*

The word *discipline*, jarred with some of those gathered. They were aghast at the possibility of being thrown out of the Church. They might just as well be tarred and feathered. Being exposed as cheats by the Reverend would embarrass, shame and humiliate them. If judged and shunned by the other members, they would feel nothing but loneliness and worthlessness.

'As I have proved to you time after time,' he continued, 'I am in direct communication with God and his Son, our Lord Jesus Christ. It is their wise suggestion, for which we must give praise, that you bring a copy of your wage or salary slips to the next meeting. Any private or state pension, or universal credit you receive, must also be declared.'

Only a few of the congregation exchanged concerned looks at hearing this. The Reverend had them too well brainwashed and conditioned. Most were too indoctrinated by his teachings and interpretations of the Bible. How could they ever question what was effectively God's will?

'This brings me to the other point I have been asked to raise. It concerns your offerings at meetings, the additional collections we make to God. Last week, it comprised of mainly coins, some of them of low denominations. So that we can avoid wasting money on additional bank charges, from now on please make sure you have five, ten, twenty, or fifty-pound notes with you. Never forget that the act of giving is an act of worship. In return for your generosity, God will provide for you.'

'Praise be to God!' came their somewhat muted reaction.

Preferring a little more enthusiasm and to ensure their obedience, devotion and gullibility, he offered them an incentive.

First, he indicated for them to be seated. 'It is your donations which pay for the hire of this hall and other associated expenses, such as the printing of flyers and other materials needed to fulfil God's work. I am excited to be able to share with you today something truly wonderful. What I'm about to reveal is at this stage still a secret, so you must keep it yourselves and tell no one else. Do you promise me this?'

'Praise be to God,' came in hushed tones.

He too lowered his voice, his reason being for good dramatic effect. 'Your tithes and donations are going to be used to start a Guardians of Modesty television channel.'

There was a round of applause at hearing this. It was not the response he was used to at Church meetings but encouraging.

'We still have some way to go,' he made a point of adding, 'but from small seeds big plants grow. One day soon, we will be sending out God's teachings not just to the people of Brighton, but to the whole world.'

They liked the idea. 'Hallelujah! Praise the Lord!'

'From our television studio we can preach why

modesty, preserved by covering the body, is crucial for spiritual purity. We can teach how nakedness leads to lustful thoughts and sinful behaviour. The vile national and international naturist organisations, which claim that nudism has nothing to do with sex, will face damnation. As Guardians of Modesty, we see through their deceit. Naked bodies, especially female ones, are deliberately aimed at temptation. It is to lure men astray, soliciting them to indulge in immoral sexual activity rather than spiritual devotion. It is plainly written in Corinthians: *Flee from sexual immorality. All other sins a person commits are outside the body, but whoever sins sexually, sins against their own body. Do you not know that your bodies are temples of the Holy Spirit, who is in you, whom you have received from God?'*

As usual, by now he had them in the palm of his hand. To an outsider, such complete control over a herd of nodding sheep might appear unnerving.

What he said next was downright chilling. 'There is a young naked whore here in Brighton who, despite all my efforts, refuses to change her ways. We can only hope and pray that she is cursed by one of Satan's evil demons.'

The congregation rose to their feel. 'Hallelujah! Praise the Lord! Praise be to God!' They had no idea who the Reverend was referring to.

Even less what he had in mind for her!

18

'I've just had a phone call from my aunt,' Liam shared, first thing in the morning.

'How is she?' Faye asked out of interest. She had only met his relative once, but she seemed a nice lady, especially as she paid their rent. 'It's a while since she's been in touch.'

'She sounded fine,' he confirmed, 'but needs me up in London tomorrow night. She's taking a new client out to dinner and wants me to meet her.'

'Is it for a ghostwriting assignment?' Faye wondered.

'Yes. The client's an American actress, who—,'

'Don't you mean actor?' she cut in. 'Male and female performers all use the same description now. It makes sense. I always referred to myself as a model. Never a model-ess.'

Her simile made him smile. 'Not this one. She's old-school and despite gender equality, still insists on being called an actress.'

Faye did not think it really mattered, if it made the lady happy. 'They do say the customer's always right.'

'Of course, especially when it comes to ghostwriting.' Liam knew this only too well, particularly from occasional clients who suffered delusions of grandeur. 'If we get the

151

contract, it'll be her book not mine, even if I do secretly write it. She's into jazz and blues and so my aunt's promised we'll take her on to a late-night club in Soho. The show doesn't start until 11pm and the place is open until 3am. It means I'm going to have to stay overnight at my aunt's. She did say you're welcome to come as well.'

Faye decided to opt out. 'You can thank her, but I'd rather stay here. After all we've been through lately, I wouldn't be the best company.'

Liam wished he did not have to go either. 'It's difficult. As we're living off my aunt's generosity, I can hardly say no, but I don't like leaving you all by yourself here in the flat.'

'I'll be fine,' she assured him, 'especially now you've secured the front door. I can have an early night and finish the book I'm reading. I'm really enjoying it.'

Despite her assurance, he was still not entirely happy with the situation. 'I'll get an early train back the next morning.'

'You worry far too much,' she scolded. 'If you're going to be out drinking all night, you'll need a lie in. Take your time and enjoy yourself.'

Late the next afternoon Liam headed off to Brighton station. He had first sought reassurance yet again from Faye that she would be okay.

Although she was not feeling cautious, she did check that the door to the flat was firmly locked and applied the safety chain he had fitted.

She then cooked herself something to eat. It was lonely to be sitting at the dining table without him.

Unsurprisingly, she took a cautionary glance at the rubbish bin, to make sure there were no rats pushing the lid open. Then she remembered that Liam had thoughtfully emptied it before leaving.

Moving into the lounge, she channel hopped the various television programmes. Eventually, she came across a re-run of the 2018 Bradley Cooper and Lady Gaga film, A Star Is Born. It had already been on for about half an hour, but as she had seen it before settled down for the remainder. It was followed by the news, which was as gloomy as ever and so she decided to have an early night.

Checking the front door again, she got ready for bed. Living the naturist lifestyle meant she was already undressed.

It seemed strange being by herself without Liam, as they were hardly ever apart. For comfort, she pictured him in her mind, sitting in a restaurant. Having no idea what the actress looked like, she visualised her as an elegant but aging blond-haired diva.

By the light of the bedside lamp, she picked up the book she was part way through. It was a fictional naturist love story, called *A Whisper in the Silence*. The bookmark showed she was a few pages into a chapter which portrayed quite a sad moment for the two main characters.

As she read the next part of the plot, her heart lifted, for love had conquered. On their private desert island in the Pacific Ocean, Ollie and Emma were dining naked on a moonlit sandy beach.

She shuffled her feet in the water, causing little ripples.

The sea was pleasantly warm. 'It's just as well I didn't wear my heels.'

'They would have been a big mistake on the soft sand,' he agreed, 'not that I've noticed you wearing them at all, since you first arrived. Bare feet are much more practical, and I am sure more comfortable. The same goes for clothes. Who needs them on such a balmy evening?'

Thanks to him, she really had become truly hooked on naturism. 'Not me, for sure. This is perfect. Just the two of us, dining like this by the water's edge.'

Faye paused reading for a moment, imagining herself and Liam in such a beautiful setting. Just like Ollie in the novel, it had been Liam who had introduced Faye to naturism.

She glanced at the bedside clock. He had only been gone for a few hours and yet she already felt an emptiness inside. He was always there for her, to look after her and to keep her safe. It was just like Ollie was doing for Emma in the novel.

She read a few more lines.

She had admittedly been glancing down at her feet every so often, to make sure none of her toes were missing. Determined not to spoil the occasion, she tried to rid her mind of sea snakes and other unpleasant things.

Faye had never seen a sea snake, except for a picture of one in a book. The mere mention of reptiles, however, was enough to cause her concern.

She wanted to read a few more pages, to find out what would happen next, but her eyelids had other ideas. It was not the story which was making her sleepy. Quite the opposite. It was simply everything she and Liam has been through in recent days. Her mind and body were nearing exhaustion.

She reluctantly put the book down, switched off the light and turned onto her side. It was too warm for a sheet and so she pushed it away.

Her hand swept across Liam's usual part of the bed. The emptiness was disquieting and so she rolled onto her back. It was not her usual position to sleep in, but at that moment felt the most comfortable.

Eyelids closed, her mind drifted in that transitional state of consciousness, between wakefulness and sleep.

Without warning, she was aware of something moving over her stomach. She had no idea what it was. If anything, it was like a heavy rolled-up damp flannel might feel.

It was being dragged ever so slowly across her skin.

Alarmed, she was immediately wide awake.

Fully consciousness, she tried to sit up.

To her dread and utter surprise, not a muscle would move. Her torso, arms and legs were all pinned firmly to the bed. The back of her head was stuck fast to the pillow. She was completely paralysed. It was as if she was glued to the mattress.

Panic set in immediately. What was happening to her? Was it a stroke? Had she suffered a brain tumour?

Whatever was crawling on her body had moved up to her chest.

It was at her throat.

With some effort, she managed to open her eyes, the

only part of her which would move.

The room was only dimly lit. The light from the streetlamp outside leaked eerily between the slightly gaping curtains.

As her eyes adjusted, what they glimpsed made her cry out.

No piercing screech emerged, for her lips would not part.

A long triangular head slithered across her face.

Scared to death, she realised what it was.

A massive snake!

Pale and brownish grey, its scaly skin had deep brown and black markings.

Its long slender forked tongue was smelling her scent.

Two round piercing eyes, each with a menacing elongated pupil, stared into hers.

She was horror-struck, her mind freaking out. No! Oh no! What kind of dangerous snake was on her? Was it about to crush her? Would it kill her and then eat her?

Other such perilous thoughts rushed through her mind. What if it was venomous? Oh my God! If so, it must have already bitten her, explaining her paralysis.

She was sweating profusely but shivering at the same time.

Dr Wright, her detestable psychologist, had once told her that such reptiles are feared by most humans. As for Faye, she was scared to death of them. Long diagnosed with ophidiophobia, the devastating distress of even seeing a snake was bad enough. If they ever showed one on television, she would turn her head away or quickly change channel. Every species of these limbless, ground-hugging serpents petrified her.

The doctor had suggested that reading and looking at pictures of them in books would be a good therapy. It had not worked at all, only increasing her trepidation. Maybe it was his idea of a sick joke.

Right now, a snake was crawling all over her.

At least her heart was still working. She could feel it thumping away like a pneumatic drill.

Wright had emphasised that snakes are one of the deadliest predators in the world for humans. He had stunned her by claiming that up to 138,000 people a year are killed by them. What if she was about to join that statistic?

From its weight alone she thought it might be an incredibly strong boa constrictor.

As its scales slid silently over her naked body, the carnivore's jaws opened threateningly. Elastic enough to engulf prey much larger than itself, she could easily be its next meal. If it devoured her a mouthful at a time, starting with her head, death would be agonizing.

She wanted to cry in pity for herself, but no tears flowed.

Instead, she made one last attempt to shift her body.

Nothing. Movement was still impossible.

Her eyes at least remained functional, but what she saw next turned her almost insane. Every curse-word she knew shot through her mind. The entire musk-stinking room was filled to the brim with dark shadowy serpentine creatures. There were hundreds of them.

The cold-blooded killers came from every angle. Most were crawling towards her. Others lay patiently still. They were in ambush, cunningly calculating exactly when to strike.

Elongated powerful pythons were climbing onto the bed, about to coil around her. Slightly shorter green anacondas lurked nearby, awaiting their turn to strangle or squeeze her to death.

Filled with hysteria, she recognised venomous snakes too. They were just like the ones in the books. She could make out their forked flicking tongues and deadly fangs.

Her hearing was obviously working. The sound of their combined angry hissing was deafening. So too was the cacophony of noises she had never realised snakes could make. There was rattling, rasping, buzzing, sizzling, popping, whistling, clicking and shrieking.

Still sweating profusely and short of breath, her throat felt choking sensations. Was it a symptom of panic, or a snake curled tightly around her neck? Her mind chose the latter.

Dangerous half-coiled hooded cobras were ready to strike from the top of the cupboard.

Red-eyed and yellow-eyed evil vipers arched on the chest of drawers.

Treacherous rattlesnakes, their tails vibrating menacingly, zig-zagged across the dresser, over her make-up and jewellery box.

A rapid black mamba sent things flying, as it weaved and pushed its way amongst them.

From the wardrobe hung at least six agile death adders,

each eager to release its deadly venom.

The snakes were ready, poised for action.

At any moment.

Now!

They all attacked her, every single one.

There was no escape.

Unconsciousness was her only defence!

19

Faye's eyes darted from side to side, up and down. Where were all the snakes?

They seemed to have vanished.

She tried to move her head to get a better view. It was paralysed, just like the rest of her. Nothing would move. Her upper and lower body and all four of her limbs were immobilised.

It was exactly as she had been earlier, when she was transitioning from wakefulness to sleep. Although she did not know it, now, as she was coming out of sleep, her level of consciousness was even more unpredictable.

A sudden onset of intense fear hit her. What was happening? She felt completely exhausted. Why could she not move? What had fate lined up for her?

To make matters worse, she felt herself sinking even further down into the mattress.

Confused, she tried to shout out, but her lips would not part. Despite being able to breathe through her nose, she still felt as if she was suffocating.

Forcing herself to take longer and deeper breaths, she managed to increase her intake of oxygen.

All the while, her mind was scrambling to try and

establish what was happening. Little did she know that snakes, symbolic of the male phallus, were nothing, compared to what was about to happen.

Her ears picked up strange auditory noises. They seemed to be coming from all four corners of the room. The combination of buzzing and grinding, whirling and whistling acoustics, were all intermixed.

Most disturbing of all was the unexpected sound of the bedroom door opening.

Who or what was entering the room?

Something heavy was being dragged or was dragging itself across the floor.

A shiver went down her spine.

The temperature dropped. An evil presence was in the room. She knew it.

Footsteps. She could distinctly hear the slow stomping of feet, one after the other. Steadily and resolutely, they were approaching the bed.

Squeezing her eyes shut was the only safeguard she could think of. It was what she had done as a child, when convinced something was hiding under the bed.

The intruder was breathing on her. She felt and heard the movement of air. It stank.

The side of the bed went down. The intruder was climbing onto it.

She held her breath at the impending danger. Never had she felt as vulnerable in her life. What was it? Why was it here? What did it want of her?

Now, it was lying beside her, an icy cold arm or

something up against hers.

She swallowed deeply. How she wished this was all a dream, but she was wide awake, fully conscious.

It was climbing on top of her.

Her heart leapt into her throat. There was so much weight on her legs, stomach and chest.

The encroacher was parting her legs, trying to get between them.

Her fear spiked, as the worst-case scenario hit realisation. She was going to be raped!

With such shocking realisation, she forced open her eyes.

It was Liam, her boyfriend. He was smiling down at her, lowering his head.

She thought he was going to kiss her, but he did not do so.

Her mind tried frantically to reason. What was he doing here? He was supposed to be in London. It must be ages before he was due back. She needed to ask.

Her jaw was still locked. Although she could not speak, he could, surely. He had not said a single thing. It was not like him to be so quiet, let alone creep up and scare her so.

Never, would he take advantage of her like this, by forcing himself on her. There was something wrong, something illogical about his presence.

Her mind pleaded over and over with him to tell her what was going on.

Not a word. Liam's face still hovered above hers. It bore a smug stupid grin. There was nothing even amusing about this. Far from it. The stress was causing her abdominal cramping. She had to do so something.

Mad with fright, she tried once more to move her body.

She cursed. None of her muscles would budge, not even the tiniest joint of her little finger.

'I… you… want,' a deep guttural drawn-out voice muttered. Although it seemed to come from Liam's mouth, it sounded nothing like him.

'I… your… body… have.' Shifting in tone, it was distorted, nefarious and sinister.

What made Liam disguise his voice in such a way? Why would he muddle his words so?

'You… mine… will… be… mine!' It was harsher, determined, even angry.

A deafening, long thundering bellow shook the room.

Faye would have jumped out of her skin had she not been paralysed. The tightness in her chest grew worse. Was she going to have a heart attack?

Trembling, her eyes looked up.

It was no longer Liam staring down at her. In his place was the most hideous and frightening face she had ever seen. With scaly red-hued warty skin, its yellow bloodshot feline eyes had vertical slit pupils. Above them, from either side of its head, jutted a large devilish curved horn. Snarling aggressively, its wide-open gaping jaws revealed ghastly canine fangs.

The forbidding demonic entity raised itself to its full height, towering over her.

Knowing the deadly peril she was in, all remaining

colour drained from Faye's face

Every one of the creature's fingers and toes had an eagle-like talon.

Ghastly and disproportioned, it was completely naked.

The most menacing and unnerving sight of all protruded from its groin.

A gigantic penis stood at full erection.

It was throbbing with lust!

Faye's darkest fears were confirmed. She knew without the slightest doubt that the savage monster's intent was to defile her body, to sexually have its way with her.

She was not religious, but closing her eyes, she prayed to any god or goddess who might be listening. Please, release my body. Let it move. She had to escape from this evil naked demon.

There was no response. She was at her attacker's mercy and still as immobile as a solid stone statue.

Disbelief at her powerless, defenceless condition, unwillingly shifted to acceptance. Even if movement had been possible, fighting back might have only escalated the crisis. She was done for. Her only option was to surrender to his might. Let him do what he wanted with her. Get it over with as quickly as possible.

Her mind wild with terror, she stared again at his rigid pulsing shaft. The length and thickness of it was spine-chilling. So too were the size of his testicles, dangling in their distended leathery scrotum.

The incubus's insatiable desire was to satisfy its depraved

carnal craving. This was the very reason it had physically manifested. All humans were its prey. There were no exceptions. Only by feeding off their sexual energy could evil spirits like this survive.

Human males were the easiest to deceive. Appearing before them as a succubus, in the guise of an attractive woman, made it easy to steal their precious sperm. The male human was so weak when it came to sexual temptation.

The female species were sometimes more difficult to delude. That is why it had first appeared as this woman's partner. Disguising the face had taken no effort at all. It was the voice which had been the problem. Pronouncing the human tongue was difficult for demons, especially in the English language. Outwitted, it had been forced to show its real tormentor self.

The debauched spirit gazed down longingly at its helpless panic-stricken victim. It wondered for a moment whether other humans found this one pleasurable to look at. Not that it mattered. To demons, appearance was irrelevant. The only things of importance were the physical sex organs and anus. The woman below him would provide him with the vagina he was desperate for.

Once connected to her, he would be able to absorb her sexual energy. He could also once more experience for himself, the pleasurable sensations of sex, which humans so loved and indulged in.

Such lecherous thoughts had stirred the creature's desires to the extreme. It could wait no longer.

Faye saw the demon lowering itself down onto her. This was no nightmare dream. She was wide awake.

Her only desire was to live. She could only hope it would do what it intended and then leave her unscathed.

As it pinned her legs and arms with its own, she so wished she could at least turn her head. The stench of its stale stinking breath was suffocating.

Her stomach churned, as she almost vomited.

Brutally, the monster forced her legs even further apart, thrusting its pelvis forward.

Demons do not embrace or engage in foreplay. Breasts and nipples are of no interest to them at all. They were simply fleshy cushions to take their enormous weight.

Faye flinched, feeling the tip of its phallus, pressing against her vagina. Having seen the size of him, she knew his penetration would be exceedingly painful.

She closed her eyes again, quivering and awaiting the moment.

With a loud grunt, the demon entered her.

Internally, she screamed and screamed. The sheer agony was even more torturous than she had expected.

The grotesque devil from hell's cold penis pushed further.

Surely, she could not take an erection this size. Whilst experiencing the extreme trauma of being raped, she feared fatal bleeding, or permanent vaginal injury.

From initial slow rhythmic thrusts, the entity's movements changed to a more desperate motion.

The bed shook and rattled, rocking back and forth, as the ghoul plunged deeper and deeper, faster and faster.

The excruciating agony was continual and absolute. Worst of all was every withdrawal. Her vaginal walls felt as if they were being scratched by razor-sharp barbed scales.

The creature's every groan grew louder.

She could only guess at the meaning of the strange words which dribbled from its mouth. They were probably hellish obscenities.

She prayed again to any deity which might exist, that the fiend would finish quickly. Her body could not endure a moment longer of its battering onslaught.

This time her supplications were answered.

With a mighty roar, loud enough to reverberate throughout the entire universe, the naked demon ejaculated.

It felt as cold as ice.

Sickened, but relieved it was over, she fainted.

When Faye recovered consciousness, she fully expected to find the naked demon still on top of her.

There was no sign of him.

In equal relief, she felt muscle movement in her body.

Tentatively, she wiggled her fingers and flexed her hands. Turning her ankles in tiny, slow circles, she found she could lift both legs.

She raised her head and then upper chest and shoulders. From there, she could sit up. Sighing with relief, audible sound now came from her mouth.

Turning her head, she surveyed the room. Twisting her body, she slowly swung her legs to the floor, attempting to stand up.

Stumbling from sheer exhaustion, she leant on the bed for support.

Gradually, blood flow restored sufficient feeling and strength to her lower limbs.

She made it to the curtains and pulled them fully apart.

Sunlight streamed in, flooding her with its healing energy.

The alarm clock radio was lying on the floor, as was the book she had been reading earlier. Some of her makeup and other things on the dresser had been moved about and a picture frame lay on its side.

There was not the slightest doubt in her mind that everything she remembered had really happened. Falling asleep after the snake attack was a possibility, but she had most definitely been awake before the demon appeared.

It had been no dream. Fully compos mentis, her brain had been fully alert for the whole time. It was only her physical body which had for some unknown reason refused to move.

Would anyone believe her, when she told them what had happened? Who would accept that she had been raped by a naked demon? They would much more likely presume she was going mad or making the whole thing up. Perhaps Dr Wright had been correct in his diagnosis all along.

Glancing back at the bed, she covered her mouth in shock. The bottom sheet was damp and soaked in blood.

She checked her thighs and pubic area. They too were bloodied.

As her hands frantically checked her intimate parts,

she was filled with repugnance. Not only was she coated with blood, but with something else.

She realised at once what the sticky milky fluid was.

Semen!

20

'So, Ms King, you've had another of your panic attacks.'

Wright was as usual so predictable with his opening words. Every single time they were precisely the same. It was as if he was quoting from the same old memorised script.

Nothing had changed in his consulting room either. It still had the unpleasant odour of perspiration.

It was enough to drive Faye mad. Her face was flushed too, as it was every time she consulted him about her embarrassing problem.

'What was it this time then?' he questioned. 'Nothing serious I hope.'

She knew he would find whatever she said laughable. He always did. 'Well, if you must know—'

'Of course I must,' he interrupted, 'or I won't be able to help you.'

She took a deep breath and whispered. 'I was attacked by snakes and a demon.' Her speech was faint enough to be inaudible.

He did not catch a word. 'What was that? You must learn to speak up young lady.'

She had no intention of talking as loudly as he did, of

telling the whole surgery. Even so, she raised her voice a little. 'I was attacked by snakes and raped by a demon last night.'

Hearing her this time, he managed to suppress a laugh. 'Really? How unusual. What will it be next time? Mugged by a monkey, or chewed by a crocodile?'

Faye found his reaction downright unprofessional. 'It might be funny to you, but it's not to me.'

Her long face revealed the sadness and frustration she felt. She needed him to believe her for once. 'It really happened. I was in bed and fully awake at the time.'

The doctor could see he had upset her. This would not usually be of any concern. He had never liked her anyway. Even so, he gave her a chance. 'You must admit that what you're saying does sound rather farfetched. Tell me exactly what you believe happened.'

She tried to explain as simply as she could, recounting the most important details.

To her surprise, he for once seemed to give a little credit to what she was telling him.

'I think you've experienced what we call sleep paralysis,' he advised. 'It's not completely unusual. Think of it as a timing error in your usual sleep cycle, which can happen at night, or in the morning, just as you say it did.'

She liked being taken seriously by him. It made such a pleasant change. 'So, what exactly is sleep paralysis?'

'Hypnagogic sleep paralysis can happen when you're falling asleep and hypnopompic sleep paralysis when you're waking up,' he pointed out. 'Basically, your mind's awake, but your body's still in the temporary paralysis of rapid eye movement sleep. It's nothing more than a harmless period of immobility, when your muscles are still in paralysis or what we call atonia.'

She recalled Jason having talked about rapid eye movement sleep, when explaining about dreams. Perhaps what the doctor was saying was connected in some way. 'Why are our bodies prevented from moving?'

'Our brain does this to us every night,' he professed, 'whilst we're asleep and in the dreaming state. It's to stop us acting out our dreams or moving our actual physical bodies whilst we're sleeping. Without this, we'd keep on waking up or perhaps in some way harm our physical body.'

'I was completely imprisoned,' she made clear. 'I wanted to jump out of bed and escape, but it was impossible.'

'Of course,' he agreed. 'Being in sleep paralysis, you felt trapped. Although you were unable to speak, you could still see and hear what was happening.'

He paused, deciding to rephrase his last few words. 'You could still see and hear what you thought was happening. The fact is, that none of it was real. You were experiencing two different things at the same time. That's all. You could see your familiar bedroom, but also the drama within a nightmare. People have reported seeing things such as you describe since at least the Middle Ages. It's often been called the Old Hag syndrome, because they felt a witch-like creature was perched on their chest.'

'It was no old witch on top of me,' she was quick to point out. 'It was a real demon. I've told you already what he looked like.'

'Let me educate you young lady.' He had returned to his old arrogant self. 'Male-looking demons are referred to as an incubus. Female-looking ones, who appear to men are known as a succubus. None of them are real, but purely products of the imagination. Hallucinations in other words.'

There was no way she could accept the last thing he had said. 'How many times must I tell you? The demon was real. It raped me.'

'Did this lead to any physically injuries?' he grilled.

Although she had at the time expected it to, the resulting wounds turned out to be emotional, rather than bodily. 'Not really, but it was exceedingly painful. I'm telling you the truth, just as I always do. The demon was real.'

He was adamant in his stubbornness. 'No. You only thought it was. Erotic dreams and fantasies are the factual explanation for incubus and succubus. Your delusion of being raped by this demon, an imaginary lover, can be put down to erotomania.'

Fay had never heard of such a thing. 'What on earth's that?'

'Erotomania,' he informed, 'is the delusion of someone being infatuated with you.'

It was obvious he was not going to believe her about the snakes and the demon, but until then she had thought their conversation had been going reasonably well. He had at least made the effort to come up with a plausible sounding explanation, even if it was probably a load of drivel.

Now, he had gone too far, saying things which were totally unacceptable.

She was not having it. 'How dare you allege that I'm deluded! You're making out it was all my fault, that I brought it on myself. For the umpteenth time, the demon was real. I was wide awake, not dreaming. As for erotomania, as you call it, if I had an imaginary lover, he'd be a darn sight better looking than the ugly brute who raped me.'

'If it's any consolation,' he offered, 'claims of such attacks are more common in people like you, who suffer with anxiety and phobias. My advice is for you to simply forget about the whole thing. It never happened.'

'I could never do that,' she made clear. 'I'll remember what happened last night for the rest of my life. That naked demon is stuck in my mind forever. Furthermore, I have proof that I was raped. There was blood on the bedsheet. How do you explain that?'

His answer was dismissive. 'From your period perhaps?'

'No way!' She was adamant. 'And what about the semen? It was not only on the bedsheet, but all over my lower body.'

A simple shrug. 'Your boyfriend's maybe?'

She could have screamed at the so-called psychiatrist. 'Liam was in London for heaven's sake. At least fifty miles from here.'

Wright's impatience showed. 'I really do have better things to do with my time than play detective with you.

Hallucinations like you had can be linked to female sexual disfunction. You probably suffer from hypoactive sexual desire and possibly orgasmic and arousal disorders.'

Her mouth gaped open. She was utterly stunned by his insinuation. 'How on earth can you say such a thing?'

'Because I'm a psychiatrist,' he reminded her smugly. 'You can hardly deny there's something wrong with you sexually. Look at the way you go around taking your clothes off in public. You were probably naked in bed too. What do you think nightdresses and pyjamas are for? You and all your nudist friends are disgusting. If I had my way you would be shot. The lot of you!'

'It's called naturism,' she fought back. 'Liam introduced me to it. It's perfectly normal, acceptable and lawful. It's also fun, healthy and in harmony with nature. What's more, it's got nothing to do with sex.'

She was of course unaware that Dr Wright suffered from gymnophobia, the abnormal fear of nudity, but his small-mindedness was most apparent.

She leant forward, her nostrils flaring. 'I know you hate naturism. You've made it perfectly clear, every time I've consulted you. There's something's seriously wrong with you and it's unhealthy. The naked human body, for some reason, scares you to death. You're the one with the real problem, not me!'

For once, he was stunned. Never in his whole career had a patient talked back to him in such a way. Not one had dared, let alone almost succeeded, in diagnosing his own traumatic phobia.

More like a psychopath than a psychiatrist, he leapt to

his feet and threw open the door.

His hand shaking with anger, he pointed a finger for her to leave. 'You're going to regret saying I've got a problem young lady. As for me being scared to death, you've no idea how close to it you are.'

His closing words made her blood run cold!

21

'It was really bad,' Faye told Liam on the phone. 'For a moment I thought Dr. Wright was going to slap me across the face. He was livid at the way I'd spoken to him.'

Liam was pleased she had stood up for herself. 'I'm sure he deserved it. He's always treated you appallingly. The man should be struck off for unprofessional misconduct.'

'As you've suggested before,' she recalled. 'I doubt he'd ever agree to see me again, should another doctor at the medical centre refer me. Not that it would matter. He's never helped me with my problems. Instead, he's made things worse. Most scary, was what he said as I was leaving. It's as if I'm paying the price, just because you and I are naturists.'

'Jason and Scarlet follow the same lifestyle,' he reminded her. 'Let's ask them what they think. You badly need advice about last night's attacks. I was worried sick when you phoned me earlier and told me about them. I felt so helpless, being in London still. Are you sure you'll be okay until I get home?'

'Right now, I'm still livid at Wright,' she admitted. 'What time do you think you'll be back in Brighton?

He disappointed her. 'It's not going to be until early

evening. The American actress enjoyed her dinner and the jazz club last night but now expects lunch. The whole thing could be a waste of time, but I've got to keep my aunt happy.'

Faye's heart sank, hearing he would be in London for a while longer. 'What if I ask Jason and Scarlet to come over for drinks about 8pm?'

It was precisely what Liam had been about to propose. 'Good idea. You go ahead and eat. I doubt I'll be hungry after a full lunch, but if I am I'll grab something at Victoria. We've still got some wine in the flat, haven't we?'

'More than enough,' she confirmed. 'It's still nice and warm down here, so I'll let Jason and Scarlet know the dress code will be naturist.'

He was pleased to hear it. 'I can't wait to get home, get my kit off and relax. All this socialising has been hard work.'

It occurred to him that his suffering had been minimal, compared to Faye. 'Are you certain you'll be okay until I get back? If not, I'll come now. Hopefully my aunt will understand.'

Faye asked him not to tell his generous relative about the snakes, the demon, or any of her other problems. 'Don't worry. I'll watch *Bargain Hunt* on TV, to keep my mind off things. It's a repeat, but one they filmed at Brighton racecourse.'

'I'll be back just as soon as I can then,' he promised. 'Love you!'

Their call ended, she rang their friends and invited them over that evening.

Everything arranged, Jason asked her if there had been any more attacks.

'I'll tell you later,' was all she revealed. She was more than nervous about having to relive the memory of the snakes and naked demon.

Liam finally got home just as Jason and Scarlet were arriving.

'My train was delayed,' he told them. 'A signalling failure, just outside Gatwick Airport. The guard said the fault was caused by a semi-conductor.'

'He must have been a part-time employee then,' Jason was quick to joke.

Although the others laughed, his humour went over Faye's head. She was too busy thinking about what she had to tell Jason.

As she was already undressed, Liam and their guests got out of their clothes too and settled down with their glasses of wine.

British summers being so short, it was good to take advantage of the warm comfy temperature while it lasted. Soon it would be far too cold for naturist socialising, apart from when the heating was on.

Scarlet was wearing a pair of novelty earrings, in the shape of mini half-peeled bananas.

'They're great,' Faye commented, taking a closer look.

'Thank you. They're fun,' she agreed. 'Regrettably, they are not one of my own designs. Jason bought them for me online.'

Liam was keen to get the conversation started. 'Thanks

for coming round. It's good to see you both again. I'm afraid to say things have got a lot worse, especially for Faye.'

Jason's memory needed a jog. 'You told me the other day about what happened on Portslade beach. Has something bad happened since then?'

Liam grimaced, glancing at Faye. 'I'm afraid so. I had to go to London, which left her on her own. She's had a dreadful time.'

Faye was trying to hide her distress.

Noticing her anguish, Scarlet gave her a comforting cuddle.

Jason looked at Faye expectantly, awaiting the details.

She sipped her drink for a moment. Taking a deep breath, she slowly disclosed everything which had happened. After describing the snakes and the naked demon, she concluded with how she had been treated by Dr Wright.

, She used the corner of the towel she was sitting on, to wipe away a tear from the corner of her eye.

Scarlet gave her another friendly embrace. 'I'm so sorry to hear what you've been through. It must have been terrifying. You should have phoned one of us. We'd have been around straight away.'

'She didn't phone me for some time,' Liam told them. 'She couldn't do a thing, until she came out of paralysis. When she did finally call, I insisted she contact her doctor.'

'By the sound of it,' Scarlet assumed,' the psychiatrist's a right bastard.'

'That's one way of putting it,' Faye affirmed, 'although

I can think of a certain four-letter word which describes him even better.'

'Let's leave him to one side for a moment,' Jason suggested. 'I think it's best if I first give you my understanding of what sleep paralysis is. Wright gave you his medical definition, but there's far more to it than that. What he said about hypnagogic and hypnopompic sleep paralysis was—'

Scarlet raised her hand. Not that it was necessary. 'Sorry to interrupt, but can you fill us in on what that means.'

Jason had forgotten he was using words that even she was unfamiliar with. 'As Faye was told at the medical centre, they're terms for sleep paralysis, which can occur when you're falling asleep at night and when you're waking up in the morning. Your mind might be alert, but your body is stopped from moving. It's a kind of inbuilt safety thing.'

'Which is basically what Dr Wright said,' Faye remembered.

'It's a perfectly acceptable scientific explanation,' Jason agreed. 'Sleep paralysis has been known about for centuries.'

'Since the Middle Ages, according to Doctor know-it-all,' Faye added.

'Probably even longer than that,' Jason estimated. 'Sleep paralysis can be given such an easy-to-understand explanation. There is the occult perspective, however. If someone wishes to harm you psychically, they might deliberately wait until you're just going to sleep, fast asleep, or just waking up. This is when your guard is down, making you most vulnerable to psychic influences. They could equally exert a false paralysis on your body, if they have the necessary skills. This is known as remote influence. It's the ability to affect a person's thoughts, feelings, actions and even physical condition from a distance. The so-called scientific experts still know very little about incubus and succubus, the demons which can attack men and women. Such entities certainly can't be dismissed as simply superstition, foolishness or hallucinations.'

Whilst listening to what Jason had been saying, Faye had also been thinking about some of Dr Wright's other absurd claims.

She thought it might be helpful to remind the others again what the psychiatrist had concluded. 'Wright told me the demons were the result of my erotic dreams and fantasies. Then he had the nerve to suggest the demon raping me was purely a delusion, brought about by my falsely thinking it was infatuated by me. He reckoned the whole thing was due to my suffering from anxiety and phobias. His most helpful advice was for me to forget about it. He was adamant that it never happened.'

'None of that was constructive counselling.' Jason was adamant. 'I'm sure it gave you little comfort. The psychiatrist doesn't presumably know much about the occult, or curses. If a person wants to place a spell on someone, they might well seek the assistance of evil spirits, or demons. This is assuming they have the power to do so.'

Liam thought back to Jason's take on what had

happened previously. 'You suspected that thought forms had been used to attack Faye in the hot tub, the naked bike ride and so on. This time even stronger forces must have been used.'

Jason was like-minded. 'Exactly. Whilst you're asleep, your astral body regularly leaves your physical body and goes on an astral journey. You often experience or remember these travels as a dream. It's on that astral level that sleep paralysis attacks take place. Demons are not of this earthly realm.'

Faye did not follow. 'Was I actually in my bedroom then, or somewhere else?'

His reply surprised her. 'We can be on more than one level of consciousness at the same time, even if we don't realise it. I strongly believe the snakes and demon attack were caused by the person we've identified as the Reverend. I'm baffled by how he was able to do so. Take demons for example. Their conjuration is usually done in a safe way by a skilled occult magician, using what is known as the *Goetia*.'

Their blank expressions told him they had no idea what he was talking about.

'The Goetia is based on a 17th century grimoire, known as the *Lesser Key of Solomon*. It was translated by Samuel MacGregor Mathers, one of the founders of the Hermetic Order of the Golden Dawn and edited by Aleister Crowley, the famous occult magician. It's a magical practice for evoking or invoking 72 different spirits or demons.'

'Are all these spirits evil?' Liam puzzled.

'Not necessarily,' Jason confided, 'except in the eyes of

the Christian Church. Traditionally, they've considered them to be fallen angels. The demons can be of great assistance to good magicians as well as bad. It's necessary to consider what is good and evil. It might help to remember that the god of one religion becomes the devil of the next. When it came to magical phenomena, Aleister Crowley never denied its objective reality. His belief was that if they're illusions, they're at least as real as many unquestioned facts of daily life. He also explained that the spirits of the Goetia are portions of the human brain.'

Faye was none the wiser by this. 'Do you mean products of my imagination?'

'Not at all,' Jason assured her. 'These demons of the unconscious mind may not be real in the same sense that we usually perceive things in our human world, but they still exist. They can appear and influence us. They are uncontrolled natural forces, related to our strengths and weaknesses and to things we crave, forsake or disregard.'

Scarlet wanted a straighter answer. 'Are they real or not then?'

'Reality is entirely dependent on subjective experience, or entirely independent of it.' He tried putting it even more simply. 'It's only when you start questioning what reality is, that you realise demons are real.'

'That's rather profound,' Liam considered. 'Can you repeat the last thing you said?'

'Certainly,' Jason obliged. 'It's only when you start questioning what reality is, that you realise demons are real. I don't want to debate what reality is right now. It would take far too long. Instead, do you have any other questions?'

'What about the snakes which attacked Faye?' Scarlet queried.

'They were there for a reason,' Jason told her. 'Amongst other things, snakes are symbolic of the male phallus and masculinity. They were also there to deliberately scare you.'

'When the demon first appeared,' Faye reminded them, 'it looked like Liam. How did it manage that?'

'By the use of incredible stage make-up,' Jason jibed. 'No. The truth is that an incubus, just like a succubus, can alter its appearance, in order to make itself more sexually attractive.'

'If that's the case,' Liam quipped, 'it chose precisely the right person to appear as.'

Faye smiled at this, but there was something she had been worrying about ever since the attack. 'When the naked demon raped me, it ejaculated. Is there any possibility I could get pregnant?'

Jason thought it most unlikely. 'In days gone by, when women claimed they'd been made pregnant by an incubus, they were often using it as an excuse, following an illicit affair with a human male. The Christian Church gave the matter quite a lot of debate. They were unsure whether human females could be fertilised by the incubus's own sperm, or whether the demon first stole the sperm from a human male. It would do so whilst in succubus form, disguised as an attractive woman. I'm far more concerned about what Dr Wright said to you as you left his office. It sounded like a threat. Our priority, however, is to work out how we're going to deal with the Reverend. We've got to put an end to his evil attacks.'

'And how do we do that?' Liam probed.

'We have to first find out who he really is,' Jason considered. 'We also need to know how he acquired such occult powers. There's an open day tomorrow at the naturist club not too far from here. We could go along as guests, as we have before. I've been told that a group of Christian naturists will be attending.'

The suggestion made Liam uneasy. He had misunderstood. 'When you say Christian naturists, I hope you don't mean the Guardians of Modesty. You told us they were the Reverend's cult?'

'Of course not,' Jason reassured, 'the Guardians of Modesty aren't naturists. They're the exact opposite. Extremists who are totally against public nudity. I was talking about legitimate Christian naturists who have most likely had a great deal of trouble from the Reverend and his cult. If that's the case, they might know more about him than we do.'

'It's worth a try,' Scarlet agreed. 'I can pick you up in my car.'

Liam had seen the weather forecast. 'Tomorrow is supposed to be sunny again. It'll make a nice day out if nothing else.'

Faye had one concern. 'As long as the Reverend doesn't find some way of attacking everyone at the naturist club.'

Jason gave her a smile of reassurance. 'Not with me there to look after you. He wouldn't dare!'

22

Scarlet's Ford Fiesta was bright red. She had chosen it for the colour. It went with her name.

After a pleasant drive the next morning, they reached the naturist club just before midday. A long narrow country lane, bordered by hedges, ran from the road to the entrance.

As they pulled into the grassy meadow used for parking, there were a good number of vehicles there already.

'It looks as if there's going to be a good turnout,' Jason predicted.

Scarlet brought her car to a halt near a tall English oak tree, so it was partly in the shade.

As the four of them climbed out, the sun shone down fiercely through a clear blue sky.

'The forecast was right,' Liam observed optimistically. 'As I told you yesterday, they said it would be bright and sunny.'

'No doubt to the Reverend's disgust,' Jason mused. 'He's bound to know about this open day and its aim to encourage more naturists. He'd probably prefer it to be pouring with rain, to put them off.'

Scarlet had started to undress. 'We'd better make the most of it then. We can leave our clothes in the car and just take our sun lotion and towels.'

'I'm going to need my phone and debit card too,' Liam had already decided. 'It's nearly time for a drink and I don't know if they take contactless payments.'

The others disrobed. It was so refreshing to once more feel the warm air against their naked skin.

'If only the Guardians of Modesty knew what they were missing,' Liam reflected. 'The peacefulness and joy of being at one with nature is so good. It's uplifting for the soul. If they were to try it for themselves just once, they'd maybe change their foolish religious misconceptions.'

'There's absolutely no chance of that happening,' Jason attested. 'All the Reverend's sheepish flock are brainwashed into thinking and doing only what he tells them to.'

They made their way over to a yellow and black striped gazebo. Hanging at the front of it was a hand-painted *Welcome to our open day* banner.

Sitting behind a trestle table, nude of course, were an elderly couple.

The man wore a grey coloured cap, with *British Naturism* embroidered on the front. The woman was busy reading *H & E Naturist* magazine. They both had healthy looking, but age-wrinkled, suntanned skin.

'Hello! It's Jason and Liam, if I remember,' the club chairman enthused. 'It's nice to see you again.'

They recognised him too. 'Hi Bill. How are you?'

'Still alive,' came his reply.

He pointed to his wife. 'You know June, don't you?'

'Of course,' Jason established. 'You've introduced us to her on our previous visits. Hi June. Keeping well?'

She gave him a smile. 'Yes. Apart from the usual old age aches and pains. The sun's a healer thank goodness.'

Liam pointed to their women. 'This is Scarlet, Jason's other half and Faye, my girlfriend. She was coming with me on the trip to the gardens. It was the one you had to postpone when the old Manor House burnt down.'

Bill lifted his hat in courtesy to the ladies, taking the opportunity to give his bald head a scratch. 'It was a shame we had to cancel. They still haven't found the cause of the blaze.'

Faye felt her cheeks tingle. She hoped no one would notice.

'There was something very strange about the fire,' Bill added. 'Amongst the ashes they discovered human remains.'

Faye and Liam, along with Jason and Scarlet, were all taken aback at hearing this.

Bill did not seem to notice. Instead, he thought to lighten the mood. 'But enough of gory things like that. You're all very welcome to our open day. Is there any chance of you signing up as members?'

Jason shook his hand, gratefully. 'It's very kind of you. We'll certainly think about finally joining, if not today then sometime soon. Just before we go and check out the changes you've made, there's something I need to ask you. Has that crazy Guardians of Modesty cult caused you any problems?'

Bill's jaw clenched in pent up anger. 'I should say so. They've brought us no end of bloody trouble. Their sole aim is to get our naturist club shut down. Several attempts have been made at putting members off attending. Only a couple of weeks ago they fly-tipped some foul-smelling liquid all over the entrance to the grounds. We can't prove it was them, but it's typical of the dirty tricks they play. We had to fork out for a specialist company to come in and clear it up. If we hadn't, there'd have been no open day.'

'I'm really sorry to hear it,' Jason sympathised, 'but it doesn't surprise me. Their leader has made no end of attacks on Liam and especially Faye. Like you, we've been unable to prove it was him. He's cunningly resourceful at hiding in the background.'

'You must speak to Paul,' Bill advised. 'He's one of our Christian members. You'll find him in the clubhouse. He's been quite successful in uncovering some useful information about the Reverend.'

This was exactly what Jason had hoped. Thanking Bill for his hospitality, they eagerly made their way inside the club's grounds.

It quickly became obvious that the committee and members had put in a lot of hard work since Jason and Liam had last visited.

The improvements were impressive. Gone was the old above-ground swimming pool. It had been replaced by an extremely smart in-ground one. What's more, it was almost twice the size. It was ideal, judging by the number of nude swimmers happily splashing about in the water.

Plentiful comfortable-looking sun loungers surroun-ded it. Most of them were already occupied by naked bodies, all getting a healthy natural dose of vitamin D.

Faye's nostrils picked up the familiar smell of sun lotion. 'If we're going to sunbathe, we'd better remember to put some on too.'

It was good to see quite a few family groups on a day out, being such a safe environment for children to be able to enjoy themselves.

Next to the tennis and volleyball courts, a rectangular miniten court had been installed. As they watched a game in action for a while, Scarlet and Faye became quite fascinated. It was rather like tennis, but without racquets. Instead, on the players' hands were double-faced wooden bats, shaped like a box.

'They're thugs,' Jason revealed.

Scarlet misunderstood. 'There's no need to be rude about the people playing.'

He chuckled. 'I wasn't being derogatory. It's what they call the special bats. This game was created by naturists, back in the 1930s.'

The grounds, surrounded by natural woodland, really were looking lovely. There were two newly mown sheltered lawns for sunbathing. A good number of people were lying or sitting on their towels. Old friends were busy talking, catching up with each other and probably exchanging holiday ideas and suggestions.

In the far corner of one field, a traditional bulls-eye archery target was set up.

Nearer, a row of wooden cabins stood next to the

large clubhouse, which was the social centre for members. Tables and chairs had been placed outside, next to a barbecue. The delicious smoky smell of charred meat reminded them that it would soon be time for some lunch.

'Let's get a drink,' Liam proposed, heading in the direction of the pavilion.

They followed him, on the way exchanging pleasantries with some of those sitting outside.

Several members were keen to tell them about some of the other facilities.

'We've got a new hot tub around the back and there's a sauna now as well.'

'If you fancy pétanque, the French ball game, it's on the far side of the pool.'

'There are some lovely walks in the woodland.'

'We have a disco here on the last Saturday every month.'

'Inside, there's a dart board and pool table near the bar.' There seemed to be so much to do.

Liam's immediate preference was for a nice cool pint of IPA beer. Jason had the same, Faye and Scarlet a frosted glass of Prosecco each.

'You girls relax with your drinks outside on the terrace,' Jason suggested. 'Liam and I need to meet this Paul, to find out what he knows about the Reverend.'

The attractive young lady serving behind the bar was most helpful in pointing out where he was.

She identified a rather skinny middle-aged man, who was sitting by himself in the corner. All he was wearing was a pair of black framed thick-lensed glasses and brown leather sandals. His thinning hair was combed over.

Walking towards him, they introduced themselves. 'We don't want to disturb you,' Jason assured him, 'but I think we all have something in common.'

'From our total lack of clothing, you're probably right,' the Christian humoured him. 'I'm guessing you might be naturists too. Are you new members of the club, or just guests for the day?'

'The latter,' Jason confirmed, shaking his hand. 'We've been here a few times before but never got around to signing up. Bill knows us quite well. In fact, it was him who suggested we should speak to you. We understand you're the leader of some Christian naturists.'

'I am indeed,' Paul proudly said. 'There's more than one such group in the UK, but we have a reasonable number of members. Most of them are here today, somewhere around the grounds. We fondly call ourselves the Christian Sun Worshippers.'

Jason was rather surprised by the name chosen for their organisation. He realised it was a play on words for Christians, who also happened to be naturists, but wondered if they had thought it through properly. A sun worshipper suggested someone who paid direct homage to the sun, or who venerated one of the ancient sun gods or goddesses. Although it might confuse some people, he decided there was nothing to be gained by mentioning it.

'It's always nice to meet people who are wearing the official naturist uniform,' Paul told them. 'Are you Christians as well?'

Jason was always open about his beliefs. 'Actually, no. I'm an occultist.'

Paul raised his eyebrows. 'So, we don't have as much in common as I first supposed. Still, each to his own. I'm not here to judge, or to convert people.'

'The term *occult* is perhaps too widely used,' Jason needed to point out. 'Although it basically means *hidden*, it's also become a one-word description for so many differing belief systems. To many it relates to the study of mysticism, supernatural or magical powers and practices. I hope you'll accept that I'm one of the good ones. I'm intent on helping my fellow humans, especially Liam, my good friend here.'

'As for me, I'm a bit of a drifter,' Liam thought to add. 'I'm not quite sure what I believe. I know the difference between what's good and bad, however. Hopefully, even that's enough to convince you we can be of help to each other.'

It was only natural for Paul to wonder what sort of assistance they were offering him. 'With the greatest respect, what exactly are you're proposing?'

'The reason Bill suggested we speak to you,' Jason divulged, 'is because like the naturist club and no doubt your organisation, we've been having a lot of trouble from the cult who call themselves the Guardians of Modesty. Their leader, the Reverend, is responsible for several serious attacks on Liam and his girlfriend, Faye.'

Paul's eyes widened at hearing this. 'I'm sorry to hear it,' he sympathised. 'It does indeed mean we have something else in common. As you surely know, the Reverend, as he so wrongly calls himself, detests all naturists. He's made several attempts to close this club. He's also viciously attacked our Christian group, branding us as heretics and deviants, just because we happen to believe in the naturist lifestyle.'

'In support of my friends,' Jason made known, 'I've found out as much as I can about the Reverend and his cult. We're hoping you might be prepared to share some more information.'

'The Reverend is a very secretive man,' Paul verified. 'The only chance we had of finding out the truth about him, was by hiring a private detective. It took him over a year to uncover the facts.'

'We badly need to know what they are,' Jason stressed. 'Without trying to sound too dramatic, it could be a matter of life and death.'

Paul looked at them one at a time, deciding whether the two young men could be trusted. Although they did not follow the same faith as him, they certainly appeared to be genuine.

'I'll tell you everything,' he promised, 'but only on one condition.'

They waited with bated breath to hear what it was.

'First, you must buy me a pint of lager!'

23

While Liam was getting the drinks, Jason popped outside to check on Scarlet and Faye.

They were both happily tucking into burgers. Neither wanted another drink. Scarlet would be driving later anyway.

What most surprised him, was how quickly the weather had changed. The temperature had dropped. Thick cloud had appeared from nowhere and was blotting out the sunshine.

'It was supposed to be sunny all day,' he reminded them, 'according to the forecast Liam heard. Let's hope it brightens up again. We won't be long, but make sure you save us something to eat.'

He went inside the clubhouse again.

'It's come up cloudy out there,' he told Paul and Liam, who handed him his beer.

'It could well be the Reverend up to his tricks,' Paul deemed. 'He's capable of doing just about anything.'

'I could possibly counter his mischief,' Jason declared.

Liam was intrigued. 'How?'

'I'll show you later,' he promised compellingly. 'First, we want to hear everything about our mutual enemy.'

Paul took a sip of his pint. 'Now I'm ready to reveal what the detective uncovered. The Reverend's real name turns out to be Blake Savage.'

Jason was impressed by even this welcome revelation. 'That's very interesting. Blake is an old English name for *black* or *dark*. Savage suggests *fierceness*.'

'Not a nice name,' Paul agreed, 'but from your interpretation it's most apt. Blake Savage was born to extraordinarily evil Satanist parents. They both possessed monstrous occult powers, which it seems their son inherited.'

Liam and Jason exchanged looks of surprise.

'It explains a lot,' Jason realised, 'especially his supernatural powers. Why though would a Satanist be so against naturism? It doesn't make sense. His parents probably carried out quite a few of their rituals naked, or *skyclad* as they would have called it. Some Wiccans traditionally do the same, as do many other spiritual seekers. It would be a mistake to consider all Satanists as being evil. The majority would probably never think of harming anyone. To avoid confusion, I'm not into anything like that. The fraternity I belong to is focussed on esoteric wisdom, personal transformation, discovering and doing one's True Will. We never interfere with other people's spirituality, unless they're deliberately harming others. We're more focussed on what's symbolised by the Rose and Cross.'

Although Paul had not understood everything Jason had said, he was about to astonish them even more. 'When Blake Savage reached eighteen years of age, his whole life and religious beliefs took an incredible turn. Some college friends persuaded him, partly out of fun, to go with them to a Gospel meeting. It was in a huge London arena and featured one of America's most credible, persuasive and impressive preachers. To their utter astonishment and to his parents' sheer horror, Blake Savage was converted to Christianity. As a born-again Christian, he denounced his mother and father and left home. From then on, he became obsessed with destroying everything which had even the smallest connection to his parents.'

Jason guessed where this was going. 'Nudity being the big one.'

'Exactly,' Paul went on. 'And it was not only down to their skyclad rituals, as you called them. As a teenager, he had unfortunately been sexually abused by his parents and other sick minded individuals. The emotional wound from such a dreadful trauma means he can only equate nudity with sex. In his twisted mind, not only are they inextricably linked, but also both evil. He really believes that in stamping out public nudity, he's doing God's will. There's nothing he won't do to destroy those who oppose him and his crazy ideas. The man's insane, a psychopath. He'll not hesitate for one moment to hurt, harm or destroy anyone who gets in his way. His sick anti-naturist obsession makes him incredibly dangerous.'

'It's worse than that,' Jason realised. 'He uses psychic, as well as psychological and physical attacks. If he's inherited extreme occult powers from his parents but has never been properly trained in how to use and control them, they are potentially lethal. It's like giving a child a nuclear warhead to play with.'

On hearing this, Paul's face went white. He made the sign of the cross. 'There's one more thing the detective discovered. It's nothing, compared to what you've just heard, but Blake Savage is also a conman. When it comes to getting rich, he's got no problem at all in conning his congregation out of all their money. The monthly tithe they all must pay, as well as every collection, ends up straight in his pocket.'

'Surely he could be reported to the police for that alone,' Liam thought likely.

'He's far too clever,' Paul pointed out. 'Believe me, we've tried, but it's impossible to nail anything on him. It doesn't help that his ever-growing number of followers believe everything he tells them. He says he's in direct contact with Jesus Christ and God and they accept it without question.'

Jason had an idea. 'There is a way we might change things. Supposing we were to stage a public meeting to debate naturism. If we were to invite his Guardians of Modesty, with the support of your Christian naturists, we might be able to break his hold over them. We need to convince them that he's a fraud and a danger to everyone. We can even invite the Reverend too. It will be interesting to see if he turns up. So, Paul, would you be willing to come along to such a meeting in Brighton and see what can be done?'

'Of course,' he agreed without hesitation. 'I'm happy to help in any way I can. When do you suggest?'

'It's got to happen quickly. I'll book a hall for the

first evening it's available. In the meantime, we'd better exchange phone numbers.'

Just then, Faye and Scarlet came in from outside.

'If you want a burger, you'd better hurry,' the latter warned. 'It's still heavy cloud out there.'

Jason dismissed their concern. 'No problem. You order the food, whilst I sort out the sky.'

Taking Liam with him, he sat down in the middle of one of the sunbathing lawns. It was almost deserted by then.

'It's not only the Reverend who can influence the weather,' he told him.

'What exactly do you intend doing,' Liam asked, fascinated. 'Are you going to bring out the sun?'

'It's already here,' Jason reminded him. 'It always has been, shining above the clouds. I'm just going to ask very nicely for the clouds in front of it to dissolve. It's a shame I don't have my tarot with me. I need to focus on the nineteenth card in the major arcana. It's the Sun.'

He closed his eyes and took a deep breath. 'It doesn't really matter. I can visualise it clearly anyway.'

He was concentrating. 'I'm going to call upon some of the solar deities to help me. *Apollo! Aten! Helios! Ra! Sol! Sol Invictus! Surya!* Together we'll first make the clouds whiter and brighter. I'm forming a strong mental image. Fine particles of saltwater are spraying onto the clouds. It's not as daft as it sounds. Scientists have been experimenting with such a technique. They call it *Marine Cloud Brightening* and use massive aerosols of sea water. I use my imagination, my image-making faculty. Brighter, whiter clouds reflect more sunlight back into space, helping in the fight against climate change. Unlike the scientists. however, I don't want any clouds at all. I'm visualising them thinning and dissipating. It will allow our Father the Sun's life-giving rays to bless us again.'

Liam could hardly believe it. Miraculously, in just moments the clouds faded away. The sky was a perfect blue once more.

'Successful occultists know what they're doing,' Jason explained. 'We always work with nature, never against it. There's a lovely Thelemic practice. It's known as *Living in the Sunlight*. Dismissing all your problems, you identify yourself with the sun and then let your own radiance shine on everyone.'

Liam could not resist a wisecrack. 'Sounds good, but right now, you're not helping much with global warming.'

'Perhaps not,' Jason admitted, looking at everyone enjoying the naturist club's open day. 'On this occasion, it's body warming I'm helping with!'

24

Their public meeting on naturism came to fruition just a few days later. Ideally, it would have been at the weekend, but the hall was only available on the Wednesday evening.

Although this left little time to let Brighton residents know about it, the night was fortunately convenient for Paul and his Christian Sun Worshippers. Bill had informed members of the naturist club, whilst Liam, Faye and Scarlet spread word to those on the naturist beach. Even some of Jason's occult fraternity wanted to support the event.

The big question was whether the Reverend and his Guardians of Modesty would show up.

It soon became obvious that at least some of them were there. They were outside the hall displaying banners. Some had *Naturists are Sinners* painted on them, others *God hates Nudity* and other similar slogans.

Anti-nudist propaganda leaflets were being handed out to people as they arrived. Despite the protestors being non-violent, a few began to shout abusive comments at those entering the hall.

Jason had a word with them, explaining it was going to be an open debate. He gave assurance that they would have a fair opportunity to voice their opinions.

By the time the meeting started at 7.30 pm it was packed inside the venue. All the rows of seats which had been put out were occupied, with other participants crammed in at the back. If the hall had an official maximum capacity, it was more than exceeded. No one had been counting anyway.

It was with some trepidation that Jason stepped onto the rostrum to start the proceedings. Sensing hostility from some of those facing him, his mouth was dry and his heart pounding.

'Good evening, ladies and gentlemen,' he began. 'Thank you for coming to our discussion on naturism. I can see we've members of organisations here tonight who hold totally opposing views. I'm hoping it might be possible to find some common ground. I'm also aware that many of you are Christians. We would have liked representatives from other religions to have been present as well but—'

A man wearing a dark suit leapt to his feet in the front row. 'There's only one true religion. Christianity!'

There was applause from those who agreed with him, but comments of scorn from those who thought such a statement inappropriate.

Jason had not expected to be interrupted so early on. Even so, he took control of the situation. With moral and religious codes clashing, the last thing he wanted was for things to get out of hand. 'Not everyone agrees with what you said but thank you for your thoughts. Are you here by yourself or—'

The confrontational character cut him short again. 'I'm a Guardian of Modesty. Our leader, the Reverend, told us that only we would be saved.'

Jason was not surprised to hear it, knowing the cult believed everything the corrupt preacher said. 'I was going to ask if your Reverend was here with you tonight.'

Blank expressions, inquisitive looking around and some shaking heads suggested not.

'What a shame,' Jason pretended. 'It would have been interesting to hear his views.' Inwardly, he was pleased the self-proclaimed minister was not there. It would make the Guardians more vulnerable.

He returned to what he had originally been meaning to say. 'Those for and against naturism often refer to the Bible's account of Adam and Eve. The story goes that—'

There was yet another angry interjection, this time from someone further back. 'A story? You make it sound like fiction. Every word in the Bible is historical fact. It's sinful to suggest otherwise.'

'You must be a Guardian of Modesty,' Jason established, 'and a literalist or fundamentalist. To ensure everyone gets a chance to speak, will anyone who wishes to do so please raise their hand, rather than interrupt.'

Several hands went up immediately.

It was not what Jason had intended and so he pressed on. 'I'll slightly rephrase what I was saying. The Bible tells us that Adam and Eve were naked in the Garden of Eden and were totally unashamed of their nudity. Tempted by a serpent, they ate from the Tree of Knowledge. Only then did they feel vulnerable.'

He was relieved to see that Paul, head of the Christian Sun Worshippers, wanted a word. He indicated for him to speak.

'Adam and Eve's sense of shame came not from their nakedness, which God had created and called good, but from their knowledge of having disobeyed God. They had eaten the forbidden fruit and then tried to cover their bodies. We Christian naturists see Adam and Eve in the blameless state God had intended them to be.'

'Rubbish!' a defensive Guardian shouted out. 'Why then did they hide themselves from God? It was because they knew their nakedness was wrong. God proceeded to make garments of skins for them. Why? Because nudity is sinful.'

Paul responded. 'God was giving them clothing for protection when they moved away from the Garden of Eden. To think he was condemning their nudity, is like saying he hated sunshine and so made clouds to block out the sun.'

Such a statement raised applause from many but also mumbled querying from the cult members.

Jason glanced over at Liam and smiled, remembering his success at dispersing the clouds at the naturist open day. They both hoped some of the Guardians might possibly begin to question their deeply held indoctrinated beliefs.

The Reverend's man in the front row was on his feet again. 'The doctrine of original sin comes directly from Adam and Eve's shameful misbehaviour.'

Of all the Christian teachings, that of original sin was the one which Jason and members of his fraternity most hated and disagreed with. It claimed everyone was born a sinner and wanted to do bad things. Such a disgusting doctrine partly explained why Jason could not accept Christianity and had sought a better spiritual path.

'This is precisely why people need to have their souls saved by God,' the self-righteous Guardian sneered. 'As for naturism, the human body has bits which are totally private and should never be seen by anyone, except in marriage. Even then, modesty must be maintained. Nudity leads directly to lust.'

Jason was determined to challenge this. 'You're so wrong. Nudity is not in itself erotic. It's a myth, propagated by misguided people, such as your Reverend. In contrast, the fashion industry's dependent on ensuring clothing has sex appeal. Clothes hide the natural beauty of the human body. As the Italian sculptor and painter, Michelangelo, said: *What spirit is so empty and blind, that it cannot grasp the fact that the human foot is more noble than the shoe and human skin more beautiful than the garment with which it is clothed.* Any Catholics here tonight will probably be aware that in Pope John Paul II's 1981 book, *Love and Responsibility*, he wrote: *Sexual modesty cannot then in any simple way be identified with the use of clothing, nor shamelessness with the absence of clothing and total or partial nakedness.*'

Paul and his supporters stood and applauded. 'Naturism has nothing to do with sex,' he emphasised. 'Someone who takes off their clothes to sunbathe or swim can't be accused of immodesty.'

'Of course they can,' another misled Guardian of Modesty insisted. 'There are regular orgies at naturist clubs. It's a well-known fact.'

Such a ridiculous claim was greeted with mocking jeers and ridicule by many.

Bill from the naturist club intervened. He was fuming at hearing such nonsense. 'Who told you that?'

'The Reverend,' several flustered voices admitted.

'Well, he's lying to you,' Bill assured them persuasively. 'He's teaching you nonsense.'

There was generally much agreement to Bill's defence and condemnation of the Reverend. Shouts of 'Your preacher's deranged!' 'He's an imbecile!' A half-wit!' and 'The man must be insane!' came from all over the hall.

'Naturism has nothing to do with sex,' Bill testified again. 'The behaviour at our naturist club is no different to clubs where people are dressed. We don't see the necessity for restrictive clothing when it's not necessary.'

Paul supported his words with another point. 'What about baptism? In early Christianity men, woman and children were baptised together naked. It was a requirement of the Church for them to be nude. The human body, in its natural state, reflects the divine and should be celebrated rather than hidden.'

There was an eruption of applause and cheers of support from all the naturists in the hall. The Guardians of Modesty were left looking at each other shame faced and intimidated. Some were questioning whether they really had been misled by the Reverend.

'That's shown them,' Liam said to Faye. 'Hopefully, it's given them some food for thought.'

'We can't be sure it's enough,' she feared. 'Can I pass on to them what Paul told you about their beloved leader being a conman?'

'It can't do any harm,' he agreed.

She stepped onto the rostrum, next to Jason.

Having everyone stare at her was disquieting, because of her phobia, but she was determined for the truth to be heard. 'There's something else you should know about the Reverend. His real name is Blake Savage and he's a conman. The monthly tithe he insists you pay him, plus all the cash from the collections he makes, goes straight into his pocket. He's stealing your hard-earned money for his own personal gain.'

Paul backed up what she was saying. 'I can confirm this. We have evidence. His hands are robbing you, whilst his mouth is filling your heads with complete absurdities.'

There were gasps of distress from the Guardians of Modesty. Some shook their heads in disbelief, but the seed of doubt had been sown.

Feeling betrayed, bitter and resentful, one by one they got up and left. Faces crumpling, countenance falling, cringing and grimacing, some were even unsteady on their feet. Heads bowed, their eyes were glazed and vacant. To say they were embarrassed at their defeat would be an understatement.

Shouts of 'Fools!' 'We pity you!' 'Simpletons!' 'Open your eyes to the truth!' and 'Morons!' followed them from inside the hall.

The man who had been sitting in the front row was the only Guardian of Modesty remaining.

He approached Faye, grabbed her hand and pulled her from the rostrum.

She managed to keep her balance, but he shoved his face close to hers.

'You've no idea how angry the Reverend's going to be.'

There was temper in his voice, but also a warning.

'He'll be absolutely furious with you!'

25

When the Reverend stepped onto his rostrum the next evening, something was very different. Most noticeable, was that he was given no 'Hallelujah' greeting.

There were also fewer Guardians of Modesty in the congregation.

None of them had their hands raised in adoration. Instead, they stood with their arms dangling heavily by their sides. Most faces bore a shocked, deeply pained expression. Their eyes stared down, fearing any contact with their leader.

Looking at them, he was amazed at his perseverance in putting up with such a bunch of pathetic good-for-nothings.

Some of them were exhausted, having not slept at all since leaving the naturist debate. Hearts saddened; their minds were confused and filled with numbed inadequacy. None of them wanted to be at the prayer meeting. Only habit and the consequential fear of not attending had forced their presence.

The Reverend had sensed something was wrong. He could hardly have failed to.

Unconsciously fondling the large gold crucifix, which

hung at his chest, he wondered why his psychic powers of clairvoyance and precognition had not warned him earlier.

He toyed with the cross again. It at least gave him the monetary comfort he constantly craved.

'We will begin our worship tonight with Psalm 100,' he proclaimed, realising the need to arouse the enthusiasm of his flock. 'It invites us to shout for joy to the Lord. So, let's do so all together, united in our faith.'

Unfortunately, after a few lines he realised he was almost singing alone. There was despondency rather than happiness in the few faltering voices he could hear.

What the hell were they playing at?

His patience being tested, he placed his hands on his hips and scowled at them, displaying his displeasure. It was crucial he kept the upper hand and treated them firmly.

'Right,' he told them sternly, 'I've had enough of this. One of you had better tell me what's going on.'

There was no response. No one dared to speak.

'At this rate we're going to be here all night,' he threatened.

He pointed to an elderly lady near the front. She had sat down, her arthritic legs making it too painful to stand. 'Why are you behaving in this disgraceful manner?'

Her reaction was to slide down further in the chair, cringing with embarrassment.

'Someone else then,' he ordered. 'One of you surely has the guts to speak up.'

Fortunately, a well-dressed man in his early twenties

had a little more self-assurance. 'Quite a few of us went to a meeting yesterday,' he admitted. 'It was organised by the naturists. We expected you to be there too.'

The Reverend had in fact completely forgotten about it but easily came up with an excuse. 'I was far too busy talking to God at the time. We had important things to discuss. Did you demonstrate outside the hall?'

'Yes,' he was told, 'before it started, with our banners and leaflets. We made certain we'd have good seats inside too, so we could put across everything you've taught us. Unfortunately, we were outnumbered by naturist supporters. They had an answer for everything. We became a laughingstock. It was humiliating.'

The man hesitated, momentarily deciding if he dare report what happened next. Clearing his throat with a nervous cough, he continued. 'They told us you were misguided and teaching us nonsense. They gave us your real name, saying it was Blake Savage. Then they really shocked us, by alleging you keep for yourself all the money we donate to the Church.'

At hearing this, the Reverend almost exploded in anger. 'Who the fu…'

He caught his language in time, rephrasing what he was saying. 'Who had the audacity and impertinence to tell you that?'

'A young woman,' he was informed. 'She's a naturist. I heard someone say her name was Faye. A man called Paul, from the Christian Sun Worshippers went on to say they had evidence.'

The Reverend knew exactly who Faye was. He was

aware of Paul's identity too. 'Let's get something straight,' he barked. 'They were lying to you. I only hope none of you were stupid enough to believe them. As I've told you before, your money's going to be used to start a Guardians of Modesty television channel. We're going to preach to the whole world, from our studio here in Brighton. 'Hallelujah! Praise the Lord!'

Rather than obediently repeating the phrase, as they usually did, the congregation remained silent.

The Reverend was inwardly a little uneasy, but he made sure not to show it. His priority was to convince them that there was no truth at all in anything they had been told. 'Those evil nudists were poisoning your minds, trying to make you believe things which aren't true. The demonic sinners want you to stop doing God's work. While your minds were being violated, our beloved Jesus Christ was telling me how proud he was of you. Your hard work in spreading his message of modesty is highly appreciated. Any public nudity must be reported to the police as a sex crime. God too wants you to do this. In return, he has promised every one of you a place in Heaven. Jesus loves you. God loves you. Never doubt it. They have told me so time after time. 'Hallelujah! Praise the Lord!'

'Hallelujah! Praise the Lord!' at last came from some of them.

He was winning them back. He placed the palm of his right hand over his heart. 'Let us pray. Almighty God, cast aside all those who indecently display their naked bodies. Destroy the whores who use nudity to corrupt the minds of men, tempting them into damnation. As it says in Revelation 3:5 *Flee from sexual immorality. Every other sin a person commits is outside the body, but the sexually immoral person sins against his own body.* Grant us the strength as your beloved family to fight the naturists. Give us the wisdom to recognise when we are being lied to by these evil disciples of Satan, so that we may overcome their deceit. Help us to never falsely criticise our beloved Reverend, who works tirelessly to serve, inspire and uplift every Guardian of Modesty. Let any moments of doubt and uncertainty be behind us. Grant us instead unwavering faith in everything he tells us, knowing that it is truly the word of God. Amen.'

'Praise be to God!' This time the response was overwhelming. 'Hallelujah! Praise the Lord!'

He had recaptured his congregation's minds and with it their faith. God may work in mysterious ways, he thought, but as the mighty Reverend I'm mesmerizing. We make a good team.

When the service was over, the Reverend returned to his comfortable flat on Brighton's Marine Parade. It overlooked the sea.

As he counted the money from the collection, he pondered on what to do next.

The naturists had, at their meeting, nearly ruined everything he had worked so hard for. Had his inherited psychic powers warned him what was happening the night before, he could have so easily put a stop to the meeting. Instead, the sun worshippers had revealed his real name and made dire accusations against him. The validity of their claims was beside the point. They had gone too far.

He detested Jason, who had organised everything, but knew he would be very difficult to attack. He possessed extremely strong supernatural powers of his own and his membership of an advanced occult order gave him immense protection.

Jason's girlfriend, Scarlet, would be easier to get at, but she was relatively harmless, only drifting along in the background.

Liam had some protection from Jason, but it was not absolute. He continued to be a worthwhile target.

Faye was the one who had stood up at the naturist meeting and spilled the beans. He had attacked her time and again, but she always bounced back, causing him even more problems. Some might admire her resilience. He hated her.

A quite simple plan to make Liam and her suffer came to mind.

He would try this first, but should it fail, there was always the ultimate choice of action.

If necessary, he would annihilate Faye completely!

26

The sun was shining yet again in Brighton.

'We're having a wonderful summer,' Liam thought aloud.

Faye strongly disagreed. 'How can you possibly say that, after everything we've been through?'

'I was actually talking about the weather,' he pointed out. 'We should make the most of it. The Met Office are forecasting for conditions to change after today.'

'What do you think we should do then?' She was open to most ideas, with the understandable exception of visiting a beach.

'How about a change of scenery?' he suggested. 'We haven't had a day out in the countryside for ages. We could go for a woodland stroll. Perhaps even a naturist one.'

They had seen naked rambling club listings in magazines and thought they looked fun.

'They're only held on certain days,' she recalled, 'and I think you have to book in advance.'

'Surely we don't have to join an organised one,' he supposed. 'There's quite a few woods and forests eastwards from Brighton. Some are part of the South Downs National Park. We could get the number 12 bus from North Street, up by the station and get off just past Seaford.'

She rather liked the idea. 'We'll need to take a snack and some water, just in case there's no facilities nearby, plus sunscreen of course.'

'And something to use as a quick cover up,' he added. 'We don't want to embarrass or upset any clothed walkers we might encounter. You could lend me one of your sarongs.'

'A nice bright pink one perhaps,' she kidded. 'You'll look lovely in it.'

He rather hoped it would be a more gender-neutral colour. 'Wraparounds would be far easier and speedier than trying to step into a pair of shorts.'

She had to agree.

The bus ride from Brighton was most enjoyable. For much of the journey they had wonderful views of the English Channel.

The route eventually took them slightly inland and in no time at all they were in the lush green countryside.

As they walked from the busy road into the peacefulness of the forest, Liam pointed to the trees. 'Most of them in this area are beech, because of the chalk and limestone soil, but we'll hopefully see some pine and ash too.'

Faye was impressed by his knowledge of the species. 'You're quite the arborist. You know far more about them than I do.'

'I'm no tree expert,' he insisted, 'but I do love trees. It's a shame Jason's not here, as he could tell us about their symbolic and spiritual meanings. The beech, he once told me, encompasses wisdom, longevity and healing.'

'They're things most people could do with,' she reasoned, 'especially us.'

He could hardly disagree, considering everything they had been going through. 'Jason reckoned their leaves are used in traditional medicine. They're supposed to have anti-inflammatory properties and a substance which draws tissue together, restricting blood flow.'

'We should make a mental note,' she said, partly tongue in cheek, 'just in case we cut ourselves.

'You never know,' he responded in mock seriousness. 'It could happen, especially when we're walking nude through the prickly undergrowth.'

Despite such thoughts, rather than sticking to the main tracks, they moved into denser parts of the forest. Not only did it give them more privacy, but an enchanted world all their own, away from the cacophony of humanity.

As they walked, the only sounds they could hear were the breaking of twigs underfoot and the calling of inquisitive birds.

Just occasionally, the sun peeped between the branches and leaves of even the tallest trees, casting flickering shadows on the foliage and forest floor.

They breathed in the captivating fresh woodland air, so much purer than even the reduced carbon emission parts of the city.

The earthly aroma of moss and soil, together with scents emitted by the trees and plants, brought back cherished childhood memories. Faye recalled family picnics with her parents; their shared laughter, playful banter, chilled lemonade and crustless sandwiches cut into triangles. Liam rekindled his enthusiasm for climbing trees; opportunities for playful adventure, daring and exploration, his imagination tapping into make-believe.

Although the temperature was expectedly lower than in the open sunlight, it was still surprisingly pleasant. Relaxed and refreshed, they bathed in the tranquillity of nature.

'There's no one around,' Liam whispered. He spoke quietly so as not to disturb the peace. 'Shall we enjoy our walk without clothes?'

'Why not?' she agreed. 'Just like we did as youngsters, before the grown-ups made us dress.'

Peeling off their T-shirts, he helped her with her bra. Then sitting on a large fallen log, they untied their trainers and slipped off their shorts. Neither had bothered to put on underwear that day.

Stuffing the garments into their backpacks, she handed him a sarong. 'You'd better have this, just in case.'

He was pleased to see it was dark blue in colour, rather than the pink she had threatened in fun. 'So far, so good. We seem to have the place all to ourselves'

She looked around again. 'Let's hope it stays that way. Just you and me, with the creatures of the forest. None of them wear clothes either.'

Their wishes were granted it seemed. An agile young squirrel spotted them and although not seemingly alarmed, darted up the bark-frayed trunk of a tree. Colourful butterflies fluttered about them, performing an intricate aerial ballet.

Faye for a moment thought a small bird had landed on her head, but as Liam showed her, it was amusingly just a fallen leaf.

After a while, they came to a clearing. It was like a very small meadow. With open sun, the grass was dry and soft and there were even more birds singing and chirping. Bees too flitted between the colourful wildflowers.

Here, they laid down their sarongs and sat eating their packed lunch. The cheese and tomato sandwiches seemed even tastier than usual. Their bottled water was by now warm, but it sufficed to quench their thirst.

Just as they were deciding whether to apply sun lotion or not, they were startled by the sound of movement.

From out of the bushes two policemen appeared.

Liam and Faye quickly tried to cover their bodies with the sarongs.

It was too late. They had already been spotted, sitting there completely nude.

The officers took a few steps nearer. Both were wearing identical uniforms; a peeked hat, yellow hi-vis fluorescent jacket and black combat-style trousers. From their duty belts hung personal protection equipment, including a baton and handcuffs.

One of them spoke into his hand-held Airwave radio.

Back from it came several beeping sounds and a garbled high-pitched female voice.

'Not what we were expecting,' Liam whispered to Faye, 'but don't worry. We haven't done anything wrong.'

'I think you'd better tell me what you said to her?' The taller policeman's tone was unnecessarily stern.

Liam wondered why he needed to know but complied with his request anyway. 'I was assuring her that we hadn't done anything wrong.'

The younger officer's chin was turned up in defiance. 'I wouldn't be so sure of that. We've caught you red handed.'

Neither Liam nor Faye had any idea what he was talking about. They were in the middle of some woodlands, minding their own business. Even so, they adjusted the sarongs to make sure they were covered.

'If you've been spying on us,' Liam pointed out, 'you no doubt watched us having our lunch.'

'And the rest,' came the reply. 'Do you always strip off naked to eat?'

'Whenever possible,' Liam confirmed. 'We're naturists.'

'So you might be,' the other one commented, 'but you're breaking the law.'

Liam decided to politely put him right. 'There are no laws in the UK which ban nudism outright, either on beaches or in other places, such as this.'

'You're wrong about the law,' he was promptly corrected. 'Public nudity is illegal if it causes distress, alarm or outrage to other people.'

'But we had no idea you were sneaking a look on us from the bushes,' Faye explained. 'Even so, I'm so sorry if it's upset you. Please accept our apologies.'

The two policemen looked at each other in amazement. 'Sarcasm won't help you, young lady. An official complaint has been made. It's alleged that you've been having sexual intercourse right here in public. Such an offence constitutes indecent exposure under the Sexual Offences Act and Outraging Public Decency under Common Law.'

Liam and Faye both went cold at hearing such an accusation. They could not believe what the policemen was saying.

'We've been doing nothing of the sort,' Liam assured them. 'To suggest otherwise is a downright lie. Who told you such rubbish?'

'We're not at liberty to disclose the complainant,' the more senior officer decided. 'You'll both get dressed and then we'll formally arrest you.'

'This is ridiculous,' Liam muttered to Faye.

He noticed that both policemen had their eyes glued on Faye. They were watching intently as she removed her sarong, ready to start putting her clothes on.

'And the two of you can have the decency to stop ogling my girlfriend's body,' he contended, 'whilst she's carrying out your demands to dress. You should both be ashamed of yourselves.'

His reprimand was not at all well received. With one of the officers blushing, they looked at each other and got their handcuffs ready. 'You do not have to say anything, but it may harm your defence if you do not mention when questioned something which you later rely on in court. Anything you do say may be given in evidence.'

'I'm perfectly happy to say one thing,' Liam declared. 'You're making a big mistake. I've got a question for you too. Where are you taking us?'

'To Brighton police station,' he was advised. 'Where

you will be questioned and formally charged.'

Faye looked across to Liam in alarm. Their arrest was really stressing her. Nothing like this had ever happened to her before.

Liam responded with a comforting smile. 'Don't worry love. Their kind offer of a lift will save us having to wait for a bus!'

27

Liam had no idea why it was necessary for the police car to have its emergency lights flashing and siren blaring. It was not exactly an emergency, but at least it got them back to Brighton quickly.

Faye was feeling even more anxious; despite knowing they had done nothing wrong.

Liam had lost more confidence in the police. He was figuring how they must surely have far better things to do with their time and resources, than believe such a false accusation. Inwardly, there was confidence that in no time at all they would be given a full apology.

When they reached the police station in John Street, the two officers discussed the reasons they were there with the custody sergeant.

Liam and Faye were then booked in and informed of their rights. Although it was offered, Liam had no interest in legal advice. He did, however, take up the offer of being able to phone someone, to tell them where they were. He chose Jason, who promised to come straight away.

Whilst waiting for him to arrive, they were at least allowed to sit together with a policewoman in an interview room. Under usual circumstances, they would probably have been placed in separate holding cells.

Faye was struggling to figure out who was responsible for causing their arrest.

Liam had already decided. He had no doubt at all.

Jason had always been good at helping people see common sense. It did not take long for him to convince the sergeant that listening to him would save the police a great deal of time.

Firstly, he explained that like himself and Scarlet, Liam and Faye were bone fide naturists. To confirm this, he persuaded the sergeant to telephone Bill from the naturist club, who had nothing but good to say about them. A phone call was then made to Paul, of the Christian Sun Worshippers, who also endorsed their exemplary status.

Most importantly, Bill, Paul and Jason had no hesitation in naming the Reverend as the person who must have made the false accusation.

The two arresting police officers had no choice, other than confirm they had not seen anything sexual. It was also established that the Reverend was not even in the woods at the time.

Jason politely quoted from the UK College of Policing official guidelines.

'As naturists have a freedom of expression,' he reminded the sergeant, 'Liam and Faye's nakedness was a lawful activity. They had not committed any sexual offences or disorderly behaviour. The Reverend's complaint should have been dismissed right from the start.'

After the intervention of a senior officer, they asked

Jason to officially join them and his friends in the interview room. There was obvious concern, but now it was about the character known as the Reverend.

'We need to find out more about this man,' the officer realised. 'Any information you can give us will be helpful and very much appreciated.'

Liam and Faye were delighted to hear that they were going to be released. They were even more pleased to tell the police everything they knew about the man who was trying so hard to harm them.

Beginning with what the private detective had discovered for the Christian naturists, they revealed his real name was Blake Savage. They told how childhood abuse had led to his obsession against naturists and his inability to distinguish between innocent nudity and sexual acts. Describing his Guardians of Modesty, explanation was given of how he manipulated the cult to further his warped ideas and steal their money.

It was more difficult for them to detail all the very serious attacks he had made on Faye, such as at the health spa, the naturist beaches, the naked bike ride and in their flat. Realising that psychic and occult powers were probably not of common knowledge to the police, they simply said that he had been responsible for many psychological and physical assaults. Understandably, they were told that a full written statement of these would be required at some point.

'I'm afraid I suffer from a number of phobias,' Faye had the courage to admit. 'Somehow, he found out about them and exploited them as a means of attack.'

'He's a very dangerous man,' Liam warned. 'He'll do anything to further his sick beliefs and ambitions.'

Jason went even further. 'Time after time I've been gravely concerned for the safety of my friends. Today's waste of police time and Liam and Faye's unwarranted arrest are nothing compared to what the Reverend's done in the past. You've got to put an end to his evil ways. If not, he'll be the cause of a devastating tragedy.'

'Leave it to us,' the senior officer assured them. 'After what you've told us, we've every intention of paying him a visit.'

'Make sure you do,' Jason advised, 'and you'd better make it sooner rather than later.'

That night, back in bed in their flat, Liam held Faye in his arms.

She kissed him on the lips. 'A good cuddle is just what I need. What a day it's been.'

'I'm sorry,' he apologised. 'If only I hadn't suggested a stroll in the woods. Maybe none of this would have happened.'

She was not so sure. 'That depraved Reverend would probably have got to us somehow, wherever we'd been.'

Liam knew she was right.

His hand gently stroked her shoulder and upper arm, as their mouths met again, this time even more passionately.

Her breathing deepened. 'Perhaps we can do now what we definitely weren't doing in the woods.'

He shared her excitement. 'Only if you want to. I was

afraid that horrible incubus had put you off sex forever.'

'Don't remind me of him,' she urged. 'What happened that early morning is etched in my memory forever. I need you to remind me what healthy sex between a loving couple is like.'

Their mouths meeting again, they explored each other's bodies, slowly and then made sensual love.

The two became one. The sun and the moon conjoined in impassioned ecstasy,

Afterwards, as they held each other in the warm tenderness of intimate affection, Liam had a question for her. 'We've been through so much together, especially this summer. I really can't imagine life without you. Would you consider making our relationship permanent. Yes, I'm asking you to marry me.'

Faye was silent for a moment. It was not that she needed time to think about his proposal. She just wanted to phrase her response in the perfect way.

'Of course I will. Was there ever any doubt? I adore you. Nothing can stop me becoming your wife.'

If only she knew!

28

'Great news,' Liam agreed on his mobile. 'I was beginning to think the American actress was wasting our time.'

His aunt had always been an early riser. It explained her 7 am phone call.

Their would-be client from across the pond was going ahead with her autobiography. Even better, she was insisting Liam had to be the ghostwriter.

There was a downside. It meant another meeting.

'Okay,' he accepted, rather reluctantly, 'I'll come up for lunch with you both, but no jazz clubs this time. I must get the train back to Brighton this evening.'

Fortunately, such arrangements suited his aunt as well.

Setting his phone back on the bedside cabinet, he rolled over, giving Faye an affectionate cuddle. 'And how's my lovely Mrs Turner this morning?'

It made her laugh. 'You're a little hasty in calling me that. You only asked me to marry you last night. First, we've got to get engaged. How do you know I'm going to take your surname anyway?'

As it had only been an assumption, he compromised. 'You can always keep your own name if you prefer, or we could combine names. Then we'd be Mr and Mrs Turner-

King.'

'Or King-Turner,' she offered as a variation. 'It sounds more regal.'

'Whatever you like best,' he assured her. 'Until my aunt's phone call, I was going to suggest we looked at some engagement rings this morning. Now I'm going to have to get the train to London Victoria instead. At least I'll be back home this evening.'

She was pleased he would not be staying in the capital overnight. She was still tormented by memories of the attacking snakes and the naked demon's rape.

Dismissing such dreadful experiences, the tips of her fingers brushed his manhood. 'If you're not too late, I'll treat you to what we did yesterday.'

'What?' he bluffed. 'Get arrested again?'

She gave him a playful slap on the arm. 'No. Silly. I meant what happened when we were back home in bed. We can make love again.'

This was a suggestion he entirely agreed with. 'An excellent idea. In the meantime, you can enjoy some window shopping for an engagement ring. If you see one you like, I can buy it for you tomorrow. They're forecasting thundery showers today by the way, so remember to take an umbrella with you.'

She giggled. 'You'd better be careful. You're turning into a weather geek!'

Mid-morning, hand in hand, they walked up to the railway station.

Giving him a lingering kiss at the ticket barrier, she

waved heartily as he boarded his train.

Her body still tingled from the ecstatic joy of his marriage proposal. She considered herself to be the luckiest woman in the world.

By the time she had walked back into the North Laine, it had started to drizzle. There could be a cloudburst for all she cared. Nothing would dampen her spirits.

Wandering from one jeweller's shop to another, by late afternoon Faye found herself in Brighton's famous Lanes. Not to be confused with the area known as the North Laine, where she and Liam lived, these narrow streets and twittens were further south in the Old Town.

Peering through a window in the pedestrianised Meeting House Lane, she finally spotted the heart-shaped ring she knew was for her. It was adorable. The label described it as being nine carat yellow gold, with cut diamonds and two small rubies. She so hoped Liam would like it too when he saw it and think it affordable.

The sky had darkened again before she was halfway home, warning of an approaching storm.

Suddenly, a taxi pulled up beside her. The back door opened and a man in his late fifties jumped out. He was wearing a very long buttoned raincoat.

'Are you Faye King? It's important I know.' There was urgency in his questioning.

As he seemed perturbed, she confirmed her identity without further thought.

He heaved a sigh. 'Thank goodness. You must come with me. Straight away.'

She had absolutely no idea who he was or what he was talking about. 'Why?' she wanted to know. 'Is there something wrong?'

'It's Liam, your boyfriend,' he told her. 'There's been a terrible accident.'

She was awestruck but confused. 'But he's in London.'

'He never got there,' came the forbidding reply. 'You must come with me now. If you don't, you'll never see him again.'

Pointing to the cab door, his other hand gave her a push. 'Quick. Jump in and I'll take you to him.'

Distraught at hearing Liam might be seriously injured, her only thought was to get to him as quickly as possible.

Once they were inside, he slammed the door.

The vehicle sped off.

As she fumbled to adjust her seatbelt, she looked again at the tall, thin, balding man sitting next to her. She could only be grateful that he had found her in time.

The journey was short, the taxi coming to a halt in a side road, just north of the station.

Aggressively pushed out through the door, she realised where they were. To her left was a hall. It was the same one Jason had hired for their naturist debate.

Baffled at what her boyfriend might be doing there, she needed an explanation. 'Why have you brought me here?'

In the absence of a reply, she was forcibly marched towards the building.

'Let me go,' she insisted, trying to break free.

The more she struggled, the more his grip on her

tightened.

She turned her head, to call to the taxi driver for help, but he had driven off.

The stranger jostled her through the entrance, slamming the door behind them.

She looked around anxiously. There was no one else there. Only seats laid out in rows.

'Where's Liam?' she demanded.

'He's not here,' the unknown person disclosed, 'and neither is anyone else. There's just you and me.'

Faye could hardly believe what she was hearing. 'But you said you would take me to him.'

The mysterious man's laughter was decidedly evil.

It sent an immediate chill down her spine.

'When I tell you who I am,' he forewarned, 'it's going to really freak you out.'

He unbuttoned his raincoat and threw it to one side, revealing a full-length black robe. From a chain around his neck hung a large gold crucifix.

'My name's Blake Savage, as you've so stupidly revealed to my followers and the police.'

Faye's heart pounded, as fright surged through her. 'Bloody hell!' she gasped. 'You're the Reverend!'

Grabbing hold of her by both arms, he dragged her down to the opposite end of the hall.

There, he twisted her around, so that she was facing the empty seats.

From his bag he pulled out a couple of black zip-tie strap fasteners.

He dangled them menacingly in front of her eyes. 'Don't even think of trying to escape.'

With unnecessary force, he tugged her hands behind her back, tightly securing her wrists together.

He did the same with her ankles.

'Set me free at once!' she squealed. 'You've got no right to do this.'

He pushed her down onto a chair. 'You're going nowhere. Just sit there and shut the fuck up. They'll be here soon.'

Who were? What was he talking about? It was unlikely that he intended to sexually assault her. From what she already knew of him, he was incapable. What then, were his intentions? 'Who are you expecting?' she questioned anxiously.

'The Guardians,' he announced. 'My faithful congregation.'

She was relieved to hear it. From what she had seen of them at Jason's meeting, they might be crazy but were hopefully harmless. It was the Reverend himself who was the danger.

Out of his bag, he took what she immediately recognised as her phone.

'How did you get my mobile? Give it back to me,' she insisted, realising the consequences.

'It was so easy,' he jeered sarcastically. 'It went from your bag to mine in the taxi. You should take better care of your possessions.'

'I want it back!' she cried, failing in her struggle against the restraints. 'It's mine.'

'Not anymore,' he taunted. 'I'm going to destroy it later. You just sit there and keep your big mouth shut. You've done me no end of harm. Do you think I appreciated the visit I received from the police? God knows how they found me, but they did. They're looking into allegations made against me, by you and your disgusting nudist friends. I've worked bloody hard for the money I've made and the respect I've earned from my flock. You've very nearly ruined everything. Now you're going to pay for it.'

He had every intention of going into detail about what he planned to do to her but was interrupted by the opening of the main door.

Members of his congregation filed in, quickly taking their places in the rows of seats.

Seeing her next to the Reverend, brought bewildered looks to most of their faces. Some of course recognised her from Jason's meeting. Others quizzed those sitting nearby on whom she might be, what she was doing at their prayer meeting and why she was tied up.

The Reverend kept them in suspense, waiting until everyone was assembled.

Only then did he step up onto the rostrum.

He opened his sermon as usual. 'Hallelujah! Praise the Lord!'

'Hallelujah! Praise the Lord!' they responded obediently.

His pride was boosted. It had been relatively easy to win them back; to dismiss the twaddle they had heard from the naturists.

'My righteous Guardians of Modesty, not only do I welcome you to our meeting tonight, but so too does God and his beloved son Jesus Christ.'

'Praise be to God!' they said as one, at mention of their deities.

'As inspiration for our fight against naturism, God is asking me to quote from Galatians.

There was no need for him to pick up his copy of the Bible. He had memorised the words he intended to convey: '*The acts of the flesh are obvious: sexual immorality, impurity, and debauchery; idolatry and witchcraft; hatred, discord, jealousy, fits of rage, self-ambition, dissensions, factions and envy: drunkenness, orgies and the like. I warn you, as I did before, that those who live like this will not inherit the kingdom of God.* This is a clear warning that humanity must abstain from immoral practices, especially from those of the flesh. The greatest evil, as we know from our continuous fight against it, is public nudity. God insists you forget everything the Christian naturists lied to you about. Nudity is strictly against his commands.'

'Praise be to God!' reverberated from the mouths of his faithful.

'You will have noticed,' he assumed, pointing at Faye, 'that we have a very special guest with us tonight.'

She pulled at the ties. Everyone was staring at her, making her feel uncomfortable. How dare he refer to her as a guest. The Reverend was misleading them as usual. She was there against her will.

'Some of you may have spotted that her arms and legs are restrained,' he calmly remarked, as if it was the most natural thing in the world. 'I have done this to protect your eyes from her shame. Had I not done so, by now she would have stripped off all her clothes, to display to you her naked body.'

Faye was not having such nonsense spoken about her. 'That's not true,' she objected aloud. 'I'm a naturist, but only when it's appropriate to be nude. Those of you who came to this very hall, to our debate on naturism, know I was fully dressed for the entire evening, as was everyone else.'

'I find what she says absurd,' the Reverend mocked, 'and so should you. She strips naked all the time, not just on the beaches, but in health facilities, whilst riding a bicycle through the centre of the city, walking the streets, in the countryside and goodness knows where else. The following words from Proverbs are most telling: *Then out came a woman to meet him, dressed like a prostitute and with crafty intent. She is unruly and defiant, her feet never stay at home; now in the street, now in the squares, at every corner she lurks.* Don't you think this describes her accurately? Of course it does.'

'How can you say such a thing?' she protested. 'I never dress like a prostitute.'

'Saints preserve us!' the Reverend implored, shaking his head in over-acted disbelief. 'Of course you dress as a prostitute. All the time. Everyone here knows the common uniform of prostitutes. It's nudity. You can hardly deny that you're naked everywhere, always on the move, searching for men who you can lure into your wicked ways. Know this, the Guardians of Modesty will triumph against you and everything you represent.'

There was a loud rumble of thunder outside. The storm was much nearer now.

'Hark!' the Reverend told his audience, his hand to his ear. 'God speaks directly to each and every one of you.'

The gullible gathering was impressed. 'Hallelujah! Praise the Lord!'

The Reverend picked up his copy of the Bible and held it high, so every single one of them could see it. 'Is this not the word of God too? As he states so clearly in Proverbs: *For a whore is a deep ditch and a strange woman is a narrow pit. Like a bandit she lies in wait and multiplies the unfaithful among men.*'

Faye was livid at being mocked so. She tried to get to her feet, but with bound legs fell back onto the chair. 'How dare you refer to me as a whore, in front of all these people. You should all know this. I'm not here voluntarily. He kidnapped me. He's evil. Sick in the head. As the police now know, he's the son of Satanists and inherited their evil powers, before converting to Christianity. He's capable of anything. If any of you dared to—'

To the Reverend's relief, a loud crash of thunder drowned whatever she was about to say. How he regretted forgetting the gaffer tape, which he had intended to gag her with.

Even a thunderstorm was not going to stop her telling them the truth. 'He was sexually abused by his paedophile parents,' she shouted to them. 'This and their naked rituals brought confusion to his pathetic mind. Ever since, he has only been able to equate nudity with sex. He can't separate the two. He wrongly believes that both are evil. He's a psychopath!'

The Reverend was fuming. She had to be silenced. 'We will now sing the hymn *Praise to the Lord, the Almighty, the King of Creation.*'

'Oh no we won't!' Faye yelled out in anger. 'You'll listen to what I'm telling you, because it's the truth. He'll do anything to destroy anyone who opposes him. It's not just naturists who are in danger from him. Everyone is, even you!'

He slapped his hand over her mouth, but she managed to bite his fingers.

As he snatched them away, she shouted defiantly. 'It's true what we told you at the meeting. He's a conman stealing all your money. He's an evil bastard.'

He went berserk at hearing her say this, belting her face so hard, that it stunned her.

Her head dropped to her chest.

The Reverend's voice rang out defiantly. '*For the lips of the strange woman drop as honeycomb, and her mouth is smoother than oil; but her end is bitter as wormwood, sharp as a two-edged sword. Her feet go down to death; her steps take hold on hell.* Take heed against her deception. Everything she does and says is false. She speaks only lies. Lies! Lies! Lies!'

The storm was getting worse. It rumbled all around the outside of the hall.

Faye's eyes opened momentarily. With a rush of adrenalin and the last of her strength she hollered, 'He's a maniac! Demented! Insane! Deranged! Stark raving mad!'

She had pushed him too far.

In a daze of fury, he picked up his bag.

From it, he pulled a gun.

Her face turned ashen at the unexpected sight of such a weapon. 'You wouldn't dare use that in front of so many witnesses,' she warned, her stomach clenching.

'You stupid bitch!' He spat the words straight at her. 'I sent you a warning of what would happen to you. Remember the doll, which the sham photographer left in your flat? The one which looked just like you. The one with a hole in its chest and a bullet inside. You should have heeded the warning then, but no, instead you destroyed it. Now I'm going to destroy you. Once and for all. Then, with you out of the way, I will come after all your naked friends. One at a time, I will wipe them out too.'

He aimed the barrel of the gun at her heart.

She gazed at it in horror, remembering how she had asked Jason if the doll and bullet meant she was going to be shot in the heart. He had said that if ever the thought came into her mind, she was to dismiss it immediately with laughter.

Try as she did, it was impossible. Instead, she begged for someone to help. Her heartbeat racing, lips trembling, eyes darting, she searched in vain for someone to rescue her. "Help me, please… someone help me… anyone… save me!'

The Reverend's eyes were full of madness. Bloodshot and narrowed in an intense stare, his eyebrows were lowered and drawn together. Nostrils flaring, his lower jaw was thrust forward, his lips pressed tightly together in determined insanity.

Realising the reality of her impending doom, Faye began to tremble uncontrollably.

Jason had once told her that we're always living slightly in the past, as it takes a while for the brain to register what's happening. It was no comfort. She knew exactly what was coming.

She was filled with sheer panic and disbelief. There was no escape. She was going to die.

The Reverend's finger tightened on the trigger.

'Go to hell, you fucking bitch!'

The deep CRACK! of the gun was deafening.

Feeling an extreme burning sensation, Faye slumped to one side, tumbling to the ground.

Unlike the myth in movies, where death comes instantly, cruelly it kept her waiting. She lay in agonising pain for moments.

Lightheaded, she was losing blood fast, her heart unable to pump properly.

Helpless, dizzy and weak, her body twitched and shivered.

Fading in and out of consciousness, every emotion moulded into one – shock, fear, helplessness and confusion.

Starved of oxygen, her brain became disoriented and detached from reality.

Like a jerky, old-time black and white film, screened within her mind, her last weeks in Brighton were speedily replayed. She was shown again the staring man in the hot-tub; the fake photographer, maggot-filled sandwiches and violent seagulls on Brighton naturist beach; filthy stinking rats in the kitchen; the disastrous naked bike ride; spiders and cannibals in the nightmare manor house; almost drowning, raw sewage and the savage dog on Portslade beach; the assault by snakes and the false arrest in the woodland for alleged indecency. Saved to last in this biopic, was the naked demon, who had so brutally raped her. Every one of these vile and vicious attacks and more had been instigated by one man – Blake Savage.

Then came a much nicer vision. It was of Liam and his precious proposal. The Reverend had taken away even this. Knowing she was dying and that their marriage would never now happen, was the most cruel and distressing realisation of all.

Her chest cavity was by now full of blood.

The crimson liquid, the vital fluid of life, dribbled from her lips.

It streamed from her chest, pooling and staining the floorboards.

Then came cardiac arrest.

As her life force faded, her body shut itself down.

Finally, the serenity of death relieved her of her suffering.

Faye King was no more.

The Reverend glanced down at her corpse with disdain.

Deciding it was best to shroud her remains from view, he threw the cover from the upright piano across her body.

He turned back to face his congregation, a wicked

smile of attainment on his face.

'The whore has gone to hell! God's work is done! Hallelujah! Praise the Lord!'

29

The Reverend had expected positive reactions from his cult members. Only someone as deranged as him would suffer such a delusion and misjudgement.

Instead, there were shrieks of horror, mortified screams and speechless disbelief.

Everyone was pointing and shouting at the same time. 'She's dead!' 'He's killed her!' 'He's a murderer!' 'The poor woman!' 'She didn't stand a chance!' 'God, save us from him!' 'He's a maniac!' 'The man's lost his mind!' 'We've been fooled!' 'Someone must call the police!'

'Bastards,' the Reverend whispered beneath his breath. How could they not understand what he had done? It was God's will. Were they too stupid to realise the righteousness of his actions? They had just witnessed him ridding the world of a sinner. They should be pleased. At least God would be delighted.

He was thinking fast, of a possible way to win them back, to really impress them. As the world's greatest preacher, he had to give them something they would never forget. They must be convinced that he, the Reverend, could perform the ultimate miracle.

There was another tremendous clap of thunder.

Even he was startled by it, but like a gift from above, it was the inspiration he needed. His greatest idea ever had come to mind. God moved in mysterious ways, but so did he, probably even more so.

'Guardians of Modesty!' he exclaimed at the top of his voice. 'The thunderstorm outside announces the presence of God!'

The hall fell silent. His plan had immediate effect.

A flash of lightning lit the windows.

'Thunder is a direct sign of his power, his glorious majesty and his firm judgement, against all who rebel against his will. He's an angry God. Thunder and lightning are also a heavenly sign of something even more important. They symbolise Jesus Christ's Second Coming. The world has been waiting for over two thousand years, but Jesus is going to return to us now. As we're told in Matthew 24:27: *For as lightning that comes from the east is visible even in the west, so will be the coming of the Son of Man.* Also, in Matthew 24:30: *They will see the Son of Man coming on the clouds of heaven.* Amen.'

Stepping down from his rostrum, with restored confidence he marched confidently down the centre aisle.

Every head turned. All eyes were upon him as he stood behind the last row of seats.

'God's speaking to me directly. He's commanding that we must all go outside. There, every one of you will witness the most important and extraordinary moment in history. You will behold the Second Coming of Christ!'

Without question, but with eager excited anticipation, they followed him out through the door. Like every

Christian from around the world, they had all been awaiting the Second Coming.

'Hallelujah! Praise the Lord!' Their enthusiasm was overwhelming.

It was pouring with rain and in seconds everyone was soaked.

No one gave it a thought. They were too busy speculating on what they were about to behold.

By now there was more than one thunderstorm. Fork and sheet lightning lit the darkened sky from every direction.

'Look up,' the Reverend commanded. 'As Revelation declares: *Behold, he is coming with the clouds, and every eye will see him – even those who pierced him. And all the tribes of the earth will mourn because of him. So shall it be. Amen.'*

He raised his arms in a welcoming gesture, encouraging them all to do the same.

'Look to the sky and let us chant together. Come, Lord Jesus, come! Mark said: *And you will see the Son of Man sitting at the right hand of Power and coming with the clouds of heaven.* Let us pray to God for his beloved son to appear. Come, Lord Jesus, come!'

Everyone rallied, repeating his calls, 'Come, Lord Jesus, come! Come, Lord Jesus, come!'

'As Jesus promised: *I go to prepare a place for you. I will come again and receive you unto myself; that where I am, there ye may be also. And whither I go ye know, and the way you know.* Come, Lord Jesus, come!'

'The Guardians of Modesty were overcome with mass hysteria. 'Come, Lord Jesus, come! Come, Lord Jesus, come!'

The downpour of rain continued to heighten the spectacle.

As the Reverend continued his preaching, he deliberately added even more theatricality. 'Revelation tells us: *He will wipe away every tear from their eyes, and death will be no more, nor will there be mourning, nor crying, nor pain anymore, for the first things have passed away.* Raise your arms even higher and plead with me. Come, Lord Jesus, come!'

All arms extended fully; their eyes were riveted on the clouds. 'Come, Lord Jesus, come! Come, Lord Jesus, come!'

'For it is written,' he avowed *The Lord himself shall descend from heaven with a shout, with the voice of the archangel and with the trumpet of God: and the dead in Christ shall rise first.* So, Come, Lord Jesus, come!'

As they endlessly repeated the call, he planted in their minds something which he knew was crucial to his plan. 'You must remember the pictures, the paintings and other images you have seen of Jesus. I want you to observe him in your mind's eye and then he will appear before you.'

Following his lead, they closed their eyes, every one of them visualising the illustrations they had seen of their beloved Christ. 'Come, Lord Jesus, come!'

'Now you may open your eyes and look to the clouds,' the Reverend instructed. 'He is here! As it was promised in the scriptures, the Second Coming is upon us!'

Eyes glaring, they saw him. He was indeed there, right before them.

Standing triumphantly, amongst the thick dark clouds, illuminated by the lightning, was Jesus Christ.

They recognised their Saviour immediately by his features - his full beard, slender pale-skinned but slightly tanned face, looking sombre but kind. His elegant long flowing dark-blond hair was swept back from the forehead and parted in the middle. He was dressed in a modest white robe, his arms open wide, embracing his worshippers below.

Most of the observers fell to their knees in veneration, homage and adoration.

Apart from sighs of happiness and wonder, they were stunned to silence. This was the greatest day of their lives.

Such an extraordinary spectacle was seen not only by those outside the hall, but soon by hundreds of surprised people around Brighton.

Word spread quickly, mainly over mobile phones. Residents and city visitors gazed in amazement.

Soon, thousands rushed out of their homes, from clubs, bars and restaurants. Shopkeepers stood outside to watch, as shoplifters used the opportunity to fill their pockets.

Traffic came to a halt, roads jamming, as drivers and passengers climbed out of their vehicles to witness such an unexpected marvel.

Some were overcome by uncontrollable emotion at what they saw. Fake news claimed World War Three had started. Emergency 999 phone lines reached crisis point.

Others simply believed it to be the most brilliant laser light or drone show ever.

Chronic alcoholics decided they were hallucinating. Drug users considered it an awesome substance delusion.

For the Christian minority, tears of joy ran from their eyes, as they offered up words of thanksgiving.

Jason and Scarlet were at the railway station, awaiting Liam. Their intention had been to have a drink together. As it happened, the arrivals board showed his train from London had been cancelled.

They looked around for Faye, expecting her to have been waiting for him too.

With no sign of her, they assumed Liam must have phoned her. If so, she would be back at the flat.

As they came out of the station, they too were utterly astonished by the spectacle in the sky.

'It's right above the hall we booked for our meeting,' Jason realised.

Hurrying up the steep road, they joined the other people gathered there. Some they recognised as being Guardians of Modesty.

Jason knew what the Reverend looked like, having spied on him at the cult's meetings. He saw him standing there, surrounded by his followers.

Instead of Blake Savage, Jason pointed to the apparition of Jesus. 'That's a sight you don't see every day,' he remarked.

'Not even in Brighton,' Scarlet agreed, 'where the weirdest and wackiest of things are quite normal.'

'What everyone's actually seeing,' he explained, 'is the imagined representation of their Jesus. It was created by Warner Sallman, the Chicago painter, in 1935. It's been copied more than five hundred million times and is universally recognised as a portrait of the Christian idol. Some have even naïvely believed it to be a photograph of him. Notice the long hair and beard. Gods of the Greco-Roman pantheon were usually depicted with such features. Their long hair distinguished them from mortals and their beards symbolized wisdom, majesty, authority and power.'

Scarlet was slightly confused. 'But you've always said that Jesus didn't really exist, that he's a mythical figure.'

'Of course,' Jason confirmed. 'If he'd been a real historical person, his hair and skin would've been much darker for a start. Aleister Crowley summed it up. He pointed out that most people, who've deeply questioned the Bible, have concluded Jesus Christ is merely a convenient title. Like a kind of hat stand, the fictional character's been used to hang the sayings and doings of other previous saviours on. There are so many similarities between the man-made Jesus and Krishna, Osiris, Horus, Dionysus, Buddha, Mithras, Adonis, Attis and more.'

Scarlet was doing her best to reason. 'If Jesus doesn't actually exist, what are we and all these other people actually staring at?'

'It's what's known as an egregore,' he informed her. 'It's an esoteric entity created from the collective mind of Christians, formed over the centuries, by millions of believers from around the world. It's fed by their shared religious belief, thoughts, emotions, devotion and spiritual union. There's not only a Christian egregore, but ones too for all the gods and goddesses which humanity has created since the beginning of time. Egregores don't even have to be religious objects. Group minds can create one for whatever they believe in. The egregore then feeds on the power of their devotees. With Satanists, for example, it would be an egregore of Satan, who is mythical too. False gods and goddesses, fallen angels and other such entities do still have merit, for they all convey important symbolism to humanity.'

It was whilst he was telling her about egregores, that one of the Guardians of Modesty made his way over to them. He recognised Jason from the naturist debate.

He was in a bad way, in a state of shock. 'That poor young woman, who was a friend of yours,' he told them. 'She's inside the hall, dead.'

Jason and Scarlet were devastated to hear this. He could only be referring to Faye.

'How can she be dead?' Jason questioned. 'What's happened?'

'The Reverend killed her,' the man declared. 'He's got a gun. He shot her straight through the heart.'

Scarlet's eyes glazed over. 'Why? What would make him do such a thing?'

'Because he hated her,' the cult member made clear, 'as he does all naturists. He kidnapped her and brought her along to our prayer meeting. When she dared to tell us damning things about him, like she did at your naturist meeting, he lost his temper, shooting her dead.'

Jason and Scarlet knew how dangerous the Reverend was from his previous attacks but were still shocked to the bone.

They ran inside the hall, dreading what they would find.

At first there was no sign of anyone. The entire place was empty.

Jason then spotted the piano cover lying on the floor. It was steeped in blood.

Crouching beside it, they lifted one end.

Seeing it was Faye, Scarlet went to scream.

Jason prevented her, fearing the Reverend might hear, even above the storm raging outside.

Without circulation, Faye had turned chillingly pale. Her face was expressionless; her muscles having relaxed when she died.

Jason pulled the cover further from her flaccid body. Her clothing was drenched in blood. The wound from the bullet hole was clearly visible.

Scarlet turned away, tears streaming down her cheeks. It was unbearable, seeing the lifeless remains of her friend.

Jason tried to comfort her, giving assurance that Faye's soul was by now in a far better place, on the astral Plane of Rest. 'One day in the future, the real spirit who was Faye, will reincarnate. Her soul will return. It will be born again in a new body, to continue its journey to perfection.'

He covered the corpse again, deeply saddened, but also angry with himself for failing to better protect her.

His real unforgiving fury was for the Reverend, who

had taken Faye's life. 'That madman has got to be stopped. He's probably still got the gun, so who knows who his next victim will be.'

'It'll probably be us,' Scarlet realised, terrified. 'We must call the police.'

'I need to deal with him first,' Jason had already decided. 'We know he's got occult powers, but so have I. Unlike him, I know how to wield them properly and safely. First, we must destroy the egregore, which he was responsible for creating with his cult members. He's using it to influence and control them. After that, the Reverend himself must be eradicated.'

'How on earth are you going to?' Scarlet questioned, with understandable uncertainty. She knew full well that Jason was a pacifist and would never willingly harm anyone.

'The forces of nature will take care of everything,' he pledged. 'As I've said before, true occultists work with nature. The egregore and the Reverend must be incinerated by fire, to avoid the shedding of any more sacred blood. Electricity is a form of fire, but lightning is far too powerful for me alone to control. I need help. The storm is a force of nature, which I must connect with on the astral.'

Scarlet recalled how he was able to control the clouds at the naturist open day. He had sought the assistance then of the sun gods. From what he was saying, however, thunderstorms were another matter entirely.

From his pocket Jason took what looked like a piece of brown glass or stone.

'This is called fulgurite,' he imparted. 'It's often known as fossilised lightning, as it was formed by a thunderstorm. As lightning blasted and discharged into sandy soil, the mineral grains fused and vitrified. I carry it during storms for protection. Tonight, I'm going to use it instead to link with the storm. Humanity has always been mystified by thunderstorms. It's why the ancients created and worshipped thunder gods, as protection and to appease such powerful divine phenomena. In time, egregores were formed of each god. These I must summon for their divine help.'

'But are they as powerful as the egregore of Jesus?' she probed.

'They're much mightier,' he assured her. 'There are far more of them. They've also been around for much longer.'

Jason sat down in the corner of the hall, facing towards the centre of the storm outside.

Scarlet could only watch in wonder as he used all the skills and occult power he had attained over the years.

Eyes closed, his mind deeply focused, he visualised each of the thunder gods, one at a time, seeking their vital assistance.

Firstly, he summoned the great *Zeus*, of the Greek religion, then *Jupiter*, his Roman counterpart.

Next came *Perkons* of the Baltics and the Celtic *Taranis*.

He invoked the Norse pantheon's mighty *Thor*, followed by *Tarhun*, king of the Hittite gods.

The Semitic *Hadad* came next, before the Mesopotamian god *Mardock*.

He called up China's *Leigong*, before Japan's *Raijin* and then *Indra*, of the Vedic religion.

Lastly, he sought help from the Aztec *Xolotl,* the Inca's *Illapa* and North America's *Thunderbird.*

Pointing his piece of fulgurite towards the storm, with all his willpower he inwardly connected with its source.

'By the sacred rites of magick and the combined power of all the thunder gods, may divine justice and rightfulness be accomplished,' he petitioned. 'Without harm to any innocent bystander,' he importantly added. 'So mote it be!'

This simply conjuration was sufficient. No further words were needed.

Outside, above the vast crowds, a mighty lightning bolt streaked across the sky.

Like a guided missile, its target was predetermined and precise.

On impact, there was the blinding flash and ear-splitting boom.

With a colossal explosion, the egregore of Jesus disintegrated into thousands of tiny glowing pieces.

Jason and Scarlet had rushed outside. They were just in time to see the last of the smouldering cinders falling to the ground.

The stunned crowd ran in every direction for cover.

The Reverend however, stood his ground in the open, cursing at the loss of the egregore.

Lightening can strike twice in the same place. Only myth claims otherwise.

A second massive bolt of lightning zig-zagged through

the sky.

With a sudden burst of light and a deafening crack, the Reverend was the quarry this time.

The lightning discharge locked his shocked body and blew out his eardrums, throwing him to the ground.

In just a split second the incredible electrical voltage had surged right through him, blistering his skin.

All his internal organs burnt.

Muscle, tissue and brain cells melted and cooked.

Inducing a cardiac arrest, he was killed stone dead.

He lay on the part-melted tarmac, his shredded clothing and chest still in flames.

The smell of smoky charred flesh filled the air.

The large gold crucifix, which he had always loved for its monetary value, had melted into a fiery white-hot twisted mess.

The Guardians of Modesty looked on, stunned and stupefied.

'It was an act of God,' one tried to reason.

'Praise be to God!' a few of them said half-heartedly.

'The Reverend's probably been sent to hell,' some supposed.

'He was there already,' Jason told them. 'Heaven and hell are right here on Earth.'

30

Liam was devastated, when Jason and Scarlet told him Faye had been murdered. Such had been his love for her, that his sorrow was deeply painful.

At first, he had great difficulty in accepting what they said. He repeatedly questioned them, full of disbelief and confusion. He was in denial that Faye was no longer alive.

When he did rationally try to make sense of his loss, he was filled with guilt. Why was he still alive? He should never have gone up to London for a further meeting with his aunt. If he had stayed in Brighton that day, Faye would still be alive.

He was full of remorse too for encouraging her to follow the naturist lifestyle, which had led to her murder. All the trauma she had suffered during the summer was down to him. Why had he convinced her that clothes-free living was normal, fun and good for her health? As things had turned out, it had been the very opposite.

There was anger too, much of it pent up inside, aimed mainly at the so-called Reverend. The appropriately named, Blake Savage, had pretended to preach the word of God, but had really been a self-seeking, cruel psychopath. His gullible Guardians of Modesty were no better, following and believing his every word without question. Why had they not intervened, before Faye was so cold bloodily murdered before their eyes?

Liam thought often about the mental trauma and physical pain she must have suffered.

In trying to find some comfort, he repeatedly reflected on his and Faye's time together, from when they had first met on Brighton's naturist beach, to their final parting kiss at the station.

He spent hours, wandering the streets, staring into the window of every jewellery shop, speculating on which engagement ring she had decided on. If he knew which one it was, he would have bought it. The undertaker could have placed it on her finger.

How he yearned for her to be once more in his arms, to touch and hold her. Without her, there was only emptiness and loneliness.

Jason and Scarlet were concerned for his mental and physical wellbeing, but he dismissively argued he was alright. Depressed and grieving, there was a vacant look in his eyes. Losing track of time, he would arrange to meet up with them, but then turn up late, or sometimes not at all.

Suffering from frequent headaches, he had trouble sleeping. He so wanted to cry, to shed tears over his loss. It might have helped, but his eyes stayed stubbornly dry.

Without Faye, their flat was no longer a home. It was an empty void. He spent as little time there as possible. As for her possessions, everything was exactly where she had left them.

It was difficult, having to explain the circumstances of her death to Faye's parents, her friends and his aunt, as it plunged him even deeper into mourning.

Although the Guardians of Modesty had witnessed the killing, the police concluded that the Reverend was the only suspect. Closure for Liam was not helped by the fact that a deceased person cannot be prosecuted.

The police did register a Recorded Crime Outcome, as there would have been sufficient evidence to charge the Reverend, had he not been killed by lightning. As Faye had died such a violent and unnatural death, the coroner still had to hold an inquest, which took quite some time.

Finally, the death certificate was issued. Never imagining her life would be cut so short, Faye had not left a will but had once mentioned a preference for burial rather than cremation.

Brighton's Woodland Valley Cemetery in Woodingdean was chosen as Faye's last resting place.

It was on the outskirts of the city, overlooking the sea and South Downs. As Liam and she had spent so much time together in these locations, it seemed a suitable choice.

A very tranquil setting, the cemetery had an eco-friendly green grass meadow, with an abundance of colourful flowers, woodland trees and wildlife.

The weather forecasters had said it would rain, but it turned out to be a beautiful sunny afternoon.

Scarlet wondered if Jason had played a hand in this, just as he had at the naturist club. When she gave him a knowing look, he smiled, knowing what she was thinking.

As Faye had not been religious, there was no formal funeral service in the chapel. In place of a celebrant, Liam asked Jason to say a few suitable words at the burial site.

Although the funeral director and pallbearers, who carried the coffin from the hearse, were formally dressed in black, everyone else was asked to wear bright colours. Faye would have wanted it that way.

Fortunately, Faye's parents were able to attend, but her mother was understandably numb with grief.

Gathered around the grave too were some of Faye's former school friends and acquaintances from the modelling profession. Bill and his wife, June, from the naturist club were there, along with Paul, leader of the Christian Sun Worshippers. Several members of Jason's occult fraternity had also insisted on attending.

The coffin was placed above the grave on wooden struts, with lowering straps through the handles. Liam had laid a single rose on it. As the symbol of love, it had been Faye's favourite flower.

Jason raised an arm in the air to get everyone's attention. 'Liam has requested that I say something appropriate. Firstly, thank you all for being here this afternoon.' His voice was choked with emotion, for he too had been so fond of Faye.

Scarlet squeezed his hand reassuringly.

He took a couple of deep breaths, regaining his composure. 'Scarlet and I had the wonderful privilege of being best friends to Faye and Liam. We'll always treasure the moments we shared. You're all, I'm sure, aware of the sad circumstances which led to Faye's life being so tragically cut short. Things were not easy for her, especially in the weeks leading up to her passing, but she always had the strength to remain positive. Every morning, she awoke with determination to make the most of the day ahead, irrespective of what might have happened the day before.'

He paused for a moment, regretting the time it had taken to discover and try to combat the Reverend's evil powers. In that, he had failed her.

Focusing on what needed to be said, he continued. 'Although Faye hadn't made her mind up about things like religion, she did like the concept of reincarnation. Also known as rebirth or transmigration, it's the conviction that the immortal soul is re-born. She was also fascinated by the dream theory of life. It's the belief some have that when we die, we wake up from a vivid, long and very confusing dream. Whatever the truth is, Faye will always live on in our memories with great fondness. Liam has decided to write a novel, in which Faye will be the main character. If the book is one day made into a film, we could all see her portrayed on the big screen.'

Liam had already told his aunt about the idea. Faye had tried many times to convince him to write under his own name, rather than anonymously as a ghostwriter for someone else. This was now his intention, as a lasting tribute to the woman he had loved and lost. He just had the American actress's biography to work on first.

'In conclusion,' Jason finished, 'we're not going to say goodbye to Faye, or at least to her beautiful soul. Instead, and far more appropriately, it's Godspeed until we meet again.'

The emotional impact of such a heartwarming thought made throats thicken and eyes water. For some at least, their grief was replaced with hope.

The funeral director signalled to the pallbearers.

The coffin was carefully lifted by the straps and the wooden struts removed.

It was slowly lowered into the grave.

Retrieving the harnesses, the pallbearers stepped away.

The funeral director passed a handful of dry soil to Liam and whispered for him to drop it onto the casket. As a sign of respect, it also symbolised Faye's return to nature.

The clattering sound it made, as it fell onto the coffin, was the cue for other mourners to do likewise.

Tears finally ran from Liam's eyes. They came with relief.

Seeing his emotion and experiencing the same, Jason and Scarlet put their arms around his shoulders in comfort.

'Let's get you off to the wake,' Jason urged.

Liam shook his head, 'No, you go on with everyone else. I'd like to stay on for a while.'

Scarlet was concerned for him. 'But how will you get back?'

'I'll call a cab,' he assured her. 'You make sure everyone gets a drink and something to eat. I won't be long.'

As the other mourners drifted back to their cars, Liam sat down on the grass, gazing into the partially filled grave.

To mind, came all the phobias poor Faye had suffered from. She had once admitted to him that she had one other overwhelming anxiety. It was known as taphophobia and was the abnormal fear of being incorrectly pronounced dead and buried alive.

He recalled too, Jason mentioning only a few moments earlier about the dream theory of life and death; how when we die, we wake up from a long, confusing dream.

Logically, he knew Faye was dead, but at the same time, his dazed mind was not sure of anything. Supposing she was only in an unnaturally deep sleep, or coma? What if her funeral and burial had been a terrible mistake?

He knew the grave would be backfilled later, after he left, but what if she then woke up?

In his mind's eye, he anticipated her horror-filled face, as she realised where she was.

He could almost hear her screaming in panic, her cries muffled by the coffin and the soil piled on top.

She would be trapped in darkness, in an inescapable box, with hardly any room to move, gasping for breath, for any remaining oxygen.

He envisioned her hands, feet and head, frantically pushing, shoving and banging at the lid; her fingers gnawed to the bone, from the friction of scraping and scratching.

In time, coffin flies would be laying their eggs on her. That once perfect body would be food for their offspring, as they developed into maggots and adult flies.

As the coffin itself decomposed, worms, ants and other insects would eagerly crawl inside too, desperate to join in the feast.

Perhaps this was all part of the hell on earth, which

Jason often referred to. Her only saviour would be suffocation.

Liam's dark thoughts were disturbed, literally. He was suddenly aware of someone standing next to him.

Looking up, he could see a man. It was not anyone he recognised.

In his late fifties, with greying hair, he was wearing an unfashionable, crumpled grey suit.

'I can see everyone's gone,' the fellow almost shouted. 'You're the only one still here.'

Liam could not understand why the stranger was talking so loudly. It was uncalled for, in the stillness and tranquillity of the woodland cemetery.

'We haven't met before, but I'm Faye's uncle,' the stranger claimed, again making too much noise. 'I know who you are though. She told me all about you.'

Liam wondered why Faye had never mentioned such a relative.

'I'll give you a lift if you like,' the man offered. 'The others at the wake are worried. They sent me to collect you.'

'I'm alright thank you,' Liam made clear. 'I'm going to stay here just a little longer by myself and then phone for a taxi.'

'There's no need,' Faye's supposed relative insisted. He looked quite put out, as he pointed down to where the road was. 'My car's waiting for you, as is everyone at the wake. It's awfully inconsiderate of you not being there with them. It's making you look selfish.'

Liam wanted to be left alone but knew there was no chance of it. 'Alright then,' he reluctantly agreed. 'If you think I should be there.'

Nothing else was said as they made their way to the car.

As they both climbed in, Liam suddenly felt something pierce the right side of his leg.

Looking down, he could see it was a syringe.

'What the hell are you doing!' he yelled in disbelief. 'What have you injected me with?'

'Just something to make you a little more relaxed,' came the reply. 'You've been under a lot of stress recently.'

Liam was enraged. 'You've got no right to inject me with anything.'

'I've every right,' came the smug reply. 'I'm fully qualified to administer drugs.'

'Not to me,' Liam protested. 'Not without my permission.'

'What makes you think that?' There was arrogance in his voice. 'In such circumstances, the injection is perfectly justified.'

Liam pulled at the door handle, trying to climb out of the car.

As he moved, his head swam with dizziness. He found it difficult to speak. 'I don't believe… you're Faye's uncle… at all.'

Of course I'm not,' came the admission. 'You stupid fool.' His voice sounded echoey and at a distance. 'I only pretended I was to get you into the car.'

His eyelids as heavy as lead, it took Liam all his

concentrated effort to ask one more question. 'Then… who… are… you?'

Even in his drugged-up state, the reply would send a shiver down his spine.

'I'm Dr Wright!'

31

When Liam awoke, he had no idea where he was. Lying flat on his back, his head and neck were supported by something soft.

He went to move his arms, but his wrists were restrained in some way. So too were his ankles.

Bewildered, he opened his eyes.

A blindingly bright light, directly above him, made them close again.

His head throbbed and he felt nauseous. Taking a deep breath, the strong smells of chlorine and disinfectant made his stomach churn again.

Turning his head to one side, he took a cautious peek. There was a door, which contained a small square window.

Glancing the other way, he could see a much larger window. It was fitted with tempered wired security glass. Beyond it was only darkness.

Lifting his head, to take in more of his surroundings, he could make out the walls. They were all painted white.

In one corner, he recognised what looked like a closed-circuit security camera. The lens was pointing directly at him. Was someone watching him? If so, who and why?

Lowering his chin against his upper chest, he peered

down the length of his body. He had been dressed in some kind of gown. White in colour, it was patterned with small grey angled squares. Lapped over at the front, two white ribbon ties held it closed.

His feet were bare, which explained why they felt so cold. Was the chilly air conditioning necessary? He wished he could turn it off, as it was excessively noisy. The annoying rattling and rumbling sound it produced was getting on his nerves. So too was the constant hum from the fluorescent light above.

As he raised his head again, he caught site of a clock on the wall. The hands showed it was 10.20. Was that morning or evening?

Another check at the window confirmed the latter.

He tried shifting his torso slightly. Whatever he was lying on made a crinkly sound. It was probably plastic sheeting, perhaps with a softer mattress beneath.

Why was he here? His instinct was to escape, to get away as quickly as he could from wherever he was.

Tugging with all his might at the straps, which secured his arms and legs, there was no give. Why was he being held a prisoner?

Redirecting his sight to the direction of the door again, he was startled to see a face. It was peering at him through the small window. Difficult to gauge whether it was male or female, it just stared. From the expression of curiosity, he might just as well have been some rare animal on display in a zoo.

There was an electrical buzzing sound, followed by a click. The robust looking door opened outwards.

Two women entered the room. The taller one wore a plain long-sleeved, full length blue dress. Her brunette hair was swept back. The second was older, with a red jumper and black slacks. Her greying hair was tied in a bun.

'Do you need to urinate?' she asked him. The sternness of her tone suggested she was not there for idle chit-chat. It was straight to business. 'There's an ensuite bathroom, but you can't use it. We've been instructed not to remove your restraints.'

Instead, she unknotted the ribbons on the gown he was wearing and opened it fully.

His nakedness uncovered, a waterproof, disposable urinal was placed between his thighs.

The younger woman slipped on a pair of blue nitrile rubber gloves.

Taking his penis between her fingers, she lifted it, positioning the tip at the opening of the vessel. Her sour face indicated displeasure for the task.

Being a naturist, Liam felt no embarrassment from his nudity. He was not however, used to strangers handling his manhood. Although he needed to empty his bladder, it was difficult, being in a lying down position, with two women watching.

Closing his eyes, he concentrated on what needed to be done. Picturing a waterfall in his mind helped nature take its course. He tried to remember when he had last used a toilet, but his mind drew a blank.

Removing the urinal, the brunette placed it on the window ledge.

'There's supposed to be three staff present in a seclusion room,' she complained.

'Don't worry,' she was told by the other, 'Dr Wright will be with us any moment.'

At the mere mention of the psychiatrist's name, Liam remembered everything. He had been at Faye's funeral, staying on after the others had left. Wright had approached him at the graveside, claiming to be Faye's uncle. Convincing him to get into his car, he had injected him in the leg with a syringe. Just before Liam had passed out, he had revealed who he really was.

Dr Wright was the last person in the world he wanted to see. If only Liam had gone into his room with Faye when she had consulted him, rather than waited outside. He would then have recognised the stranger at the cemetery.

Knowing he was about to come face to face with him again, he pleaded for the women's help. 'You've got to get me out of here,' he begged, 'before that madman arrives. God knows what he's up to.'

The two ladies gave each other a nonchalant look. Ridiculous comments like this were quite common from patients in their care. It was, after all, that kind of place.

The lock on the door buzzed again and in breezed Dr Wright. He had a satisfied smile on his face but smelled of perspiration.

Liam wrestled with the restraining straps again. 'Let me go!' he demanded. 'You've abducted me.'

The doctor sat down on the side of the bed. His put-on demeanour was more like a friendly relative who had come to visit.

'*Abducted* is not quite the right word, Liam. You've been detained, or sectioned as we call it, under the Mental Health Act.' He was talking in a much quieter and relaxed way than he had been at the cemetery.

Liam assumed it was to ensure he was not overheard.

'It's for your own safety and for the protection of those around you,' he disclosed. 'This is a psychiatric hospital, but you're extremely privileged. You've been given your own private room.'

'My safety, which you're referring to,' Liam pointed out, 'would be much greater if I was in the open, surrounded by sane people.'

Wright sighed disparagingly. 'You're much better off in this room, rather than a general ward. You'd find it much too noisy. They're full of patients talking to themselves, humming, whistling and singing loudly. The quieter ones just stare out of the windows, or walk backwards and forwards day and night, muttering incoherently. Quite a few cry their eyes out for no apparent reason. Others suddenly start to scream. Then there's the alarms. There's at least one going off at any given time. With the overworked nurses and other staff rushed off their feet, they never get time to answer the phones. They're ringing constantly and would keep you awake. There are so many unpleasant smells too, of vomit, urine, faeces, sweat and bleach. This room, by comparison, is a haven of serenity. There's no possibility at all of us being disturbed.'

It was the last thing he said which most scared Liam. The reason for his isolation was more likely to stop him telling the world how evil Dr Wright was. Even worse, it could be to keep secret whatever the maniac intended to do.

'You had no right to drug me and bring me here,' he asserted. 'I demand you set me free at once.'

Wright threw his head back in laughter. 'You really don't understand, do you? You have no right at all to leave, or to refuse any treatment I decide to give you.'

'I must have,' Liam tried to reason. 'There must be laws to protect innocent people like me.'

The doctor raised his chin in stubbornness. 'You could I suppose appeal to the Mental Health Tribunal against your section. Unfortunately, it would take six to eight weeks from your appeal being submitted. So, it's not an option. You're not going to be around for that long.'

It was again his final few words which were the most startling. Did he mean not going to be around for long in the hospital, or something far more sinister?

Wright got to his feet. 'We need to get on with your treatment. I haven't got all night. Any negativity on your part is purely your reaction to being in seclusion. It can make you feel angry, or sad, hopeless and vulnerable.'

'All of those emotions,' Liam reminded him, 'are what you inflicted on Faye. Whenever she consulted you, she left feeling that way. Why didn't you make any effort to help her? Why couldn't you have done something to sort out her phobias and other problems?'

His reply came as a complete surprise. 'It was not in my interest to do so. We needed to use her weaknesses as a way of getting at her. We were trying to break her down, into total submission. We had to persuade her to give up all that stupid nonsense of naturism.'

Liam was dumbfounded at this admission. 'When you say *we*, who are you referring to?'

'It was someone you never met,' Wright came clean. 'Faye did however, which led to her death. His name was Blake Savage, but he was better known as the Reverend.'

'You bastard!' Liam hollered. 'Faye came to you for help with her panic attacks. You were supposed to come up with a treatment plan. Instead, you collaborated with a psychopath, passing on personal and confidential medical information.'

From his arrogant expression, Wright was proud of his achievements. He had obviously taken pride in deceiving her. 'Faye was far too naïve to guess what I was doing.'

'But what made you do it?' Liam failed to comprehend. 'What was in it for you?'

'The Guardians of Modesty,' he proclaimed. 'The religious organisation was started by me. It's my movement, part of my campaign against public nudity. I've always hated the concept of nudism. The naked human body is vulgar and should never be exposed to view. Doing so is a disgrace. If I had my way, every one of you would be sectioned.'

Like Faye, Liam had no idea that the doctor had been mocked and bullied from childhood, because of his psoriasis, leading to his fear of nudity.

Wright was telling no one about his own mental phobia. It was none of their business. As an adult it had almost ruined his life. The Reverend had been perfectly right. Nudity and sex could not be separated, even if others were too blind to see it.

If only Liam and his friends had suspected Wright's involvement with the Reverend. They could have done so much more to protect Faye. She would probably have still been alive.

He spat at the detestable man. 'You're morally depraved. It was your degenerate mind and diabolic betrayal of medical oaths and ethics which cost Faye her life. The one small consolation is that your Guardians of Modesty are finished, now the Reverend's dead.'

The slow side-to-side movements of his head said otherwise. 'Not at all. I'm in the process of finding a new preacher. Blake Savage had incredible powers and skills. He was exceptional. I particularly liked the time he conjured a naked demon to attack Faye.'

Liam was again stunned at such an admission. 'You enjoyed such extreme cruelty? The evil entity brutally raped her.'

Wright dismissed what he said with a mere wave of the hand. 'It had to be done. Sex and nudity are inseparable. They're also detestable, which made Faye responsible for her own suffering. The Reverend was serving God. It's why his followers believed every word he told them. He'll be greatly missed, but there are many other preachers out there I can appoint. I just need to make sure the next Reverend is not the sort who sticks their fingers in the till.'

Liam glared at both nurses. They had been standing, listening to the conversation, without the slightest concern.

'What about these two? They've heard everything you've told me. They could easily report you to the police, as the Reverend's employer. You could be imprisoned for aiding him in Faye's murder.'

Wright smiled at the ladies with fondness. 'It's most unlikely. They're both extremely loyal and dedicated Guardians of Modesty. I trust them fully.'

'Hallelujah! Praise the Lord!' the two of them intoned in unison.

It was almost enough to make Liam vomit.

In desperation, he pointed to the CCTV camera on the wall. 'What about that? Everything you've said will have been recorded.'

Dr Wright knew otherwise 'You're so easily taken in. Don't you read the newspapers or watch the television news? The National Health Service is almost bankrupt. It's on its knees. The security camera hasn't worked for years. I doubt there's one in the entire hospital which functions.'

Liam felt real panic. Never had he felt so defenceless. His skin was flushed, and he was perspiring heavily, despite the cold. He was trapped in the room with a man as psychotic as the Reverend had been. He feared for his life.

'Enough of this friendly gossip,' the doctor decided. 'It's time to get on with the job. We need to carry out a procedure. It'll stop you from taking your clothes off in public once and for all. In the good old days, doctors would have been allowed to initially use electro-shock treatment. Sadly, they've stopped us from doing so, officially anyway. It's quite a shame really. There are fascinating reports and studies, showing how the voltage made the patient's body contract into the most intriguing positions. Rubber wedges were placed in the mouth, to stop them biting their tongue off, but teeth would still break and bones and ligaments snap. Goodness knows why the authorities stopped such fun!'

Liam was trembling from head to toe. 'What are you intending to do to me?'

'It's a very simple intervention,' the doctor calmly informed him. 'It'll only take a moment.'

'But you're a psychiatrist,' Liam reminded him in desperation.

'And you're a naturist,' Wright countered. 'Not a normal civilised human being.'

He gestured for one of the nurses to open the front of the robe Liam was wearing.

As she did so, the doctor caught first sight of Liam's genitals. His face grimaced in disgust. 'What a horrible sight. I so hate the naked human body. This is going to be almost as painful for me as it will be for you.'

He and the older nurse put on their surgical gloves.

'Are we giving him an anaesthetic?' she asked

'No, it won't be necessary,' Wright had already decided. 'By the way, I deliberately gave him a very large dose of blood thinners when he was first brought here. So, expect a lot of mess. Pass me the scalpel please.'

Liam's pulse pounded in his ears. The mere sight of the shiny stainless steel cutting tool made his abdomen cramp.

The doctor pointed the tip of the blade at him, making

threatening cutting motions in the air.

Flight response kicking in, Liam tugged hopelessly at the straps holding him down. 'You're as mad as the Reverend was. Insane!'

'I don't want to touch his penis, even with gloves on,' the doctor told the other nurse. 'Perhaps you could oblige by holding it upwards.'

The blunt side of the scalpel was run across his manhood, the best angle being decided upon.

Liam felt the coldness of the metal on his sensitive skin.

His whole body jerked.

'My preference is to slice straight through the flesh, here at the base,' the maniac had worked out. 'The scalpel is incredibly sharp.'

'Help me, please… someone help me!' Liam shrieked.

Little did he know that these were precisely the same words Faye had pleaded, just before she was shot dead by the Reverend.

In desperation, his eyes darted around the room for assistance. There was none. The seclusion room was surely soundproofed. The small window in the door had been covered and the blind closed over the large one.

Liam thought of his friend, Jason, but knew he would have no idea of where he was. The Guardians of Modesty would be of no more help than they had been to Faye.

Hiding his fear would be the manly thing to do, but it was impossible.

Gasping for air, he tried to draw a full breath.

Looking down, he saw Wright's hands trembling.

Slowly, the scalpel was turned over, the razor-sharp blade ready.

It touched the side of his penis.

In tormented horror Liam squeezed his eyes shut.

Then, he screamed at the top of his voice.

'NOOOOOOOO!'